LIFE UPCYCLED

A HEARTWARMING JOURNEY

CARMEN KLASSEN

ETA Publishing Ltd

CHAPTER 1

"Matthew! Please!" Carrie tried to connect with her son, to somehow make him see that this was all wrong and that she loved him and his sister more than anything. But his steely glare didn't change. He started to pull Katie away.

"Katie-girl, you know I love you!" But Katie, too, couldn't be reached. She wasn't even looking at her mom. Instead she was turning towards her Dad—the man she had always been scared of—and getting ready to follow her brother into a dirty-looking van with dark windows.

"It's over now Carrie," Don sneered, his hand gripped tight on Matthew's shoulder. "I never forget when someone screws me over. Say goodbye to your precious little babies. When I'm done with them, they won't even remember you."

"NO!"

Carrie gasped as she woke up. Her heart was beating so hard it was causing her physical pain, and she felt like her spirit had been shattered into a thousand pieces. She looked over at Katie, worried she had cried out loud and woken her up. But Katie was still sound asleep in her bed next to the mattress Carrie slept on. Quickly Carrie slipped out of the room and went downstairs to her favorite armchair.

She wrapped a blanket around herself and tried to breathe deeply to calm her pounding heart, but every breath felt like it would crack her ribs. "What the heck?" she whispered as she looked up at the ceiling. This was the third nightmare in a row. In each one her ex-husband Don was taking her kids away—and the kids wanted to leave.

It made no sense. Why now? She was supposed to be happy! For the first time, she was making enough money to support herself and the kids. Don was in prison and still had another year to serve on a drunk driving conviction. The divorce was final, and she was starting grad school in September. Everything in her life was better than it had ever been. So why was she getting such terrible nightmares?

She didn't know how long she sat there, trying to reign in the panic her nightmare had created. Finally, she dragged herself up to bed, knowing sleep wouldn't come easily, and tomorrow she'd have to face the day and pretend that everything was fine...

Carrie slowly opened her eyes. The sun was bright through the cheap blinds that covered her bedroom window. Rolling over she glanced up at Katie and breathed a sigh of relief. It *was* just a dream. Katie had one arm and one leg hanging over the edge of the bed—classic positioning for the five year old who was full of personality, even when she slept. Her heart softened with relief. Last night was not real. Katie and Matthew were still here, and they still loved her.

Walking gently down the worn and stained stairs, she tried to ignore the tired, drab feel in her townhouse. As a single mom and a full-time student, she needed the subsidized housing, even if it meant sharing a bedroom with her daughter and living with 1980s paint and floor-ing. But the way she was feeling right now it was hard to appreciate it.

She kissed Matthew on his forehead but resisted the urge to gather him into her arms like she did when he was a toddler and just hold onto him. He was on the couch in their small living room, playing on his Nintendo Switch. In the kitchen Carrie slipped a French Roast coffee pod into her coffee maker and inhaled the aroma as her coffee brewed. Having decent coffee was a luxury that she never took for granted.

It wasn't that long ago that she had been struggling to buy even the most basic groceries. Things were much better now. Her side business creatively refinishing picture frames—along with a packet of cash she found wedged in the drawer of an abandoned side table—had allowed her to finish her undergrad psychology degree. Now she just had to focus on earning enough money to pay for her first year of grad school.

She took her coffee to the living room and sat with Matthew. The early weekend mornings were usually 'their' time before the tiny hurricane that was Katie joined them. They didn't often talk, but just being together was nice. If only she could shake the lingering darkness of her nightmares that kept all of her worries company as they rattled through her mind.

Even though all she wanted was to gather up Matthew and Katie and run away until the nightmares couldn't reach her, she had to get a grip—or at least look like she had a grip. It was a week since she had taken her last undergrad exam. In three more months she needed to have $9,000 to pay for her first year of grad school, or she'd be stuck delaying her career plans for another year. Getting her master's degree and becoming a counselling psychologist was a dream she had carried since high school, but it still seemed hard to believe that she might actually get there.

Katie's arrival downstairs forced Carrie out of her thoughts.

"Good morning Katie-girl!"

Katie climbed into Carrie's lap and snuggled in. Her brown curly hair stuck out in every direction, and her eyes were still half closed. Carrie wrapped her arms around her daughter and breathed in her little-girl smell. A very busy five-year-old, her snuggle times were rare and Carrie cherished every one. It felt especially meaningful after last night's horrible dream. Less than two minutes later Katie had completely woken up and was raring to go.

"Is it time for my soccer game yet Mommy? We should eat breakfast! Can we get ice cream after? And is Angela coming today?"

"Let's see…" Carrie held up her phone and showed Katie the time. "It's 8:34, so we still have more than an hour before it's time to go to your game. We can eat breakfast whenever you want. We'll only go out for ice cream if the rest of the team goes, and it's still two more days until Angela starts coming over to our place after school. Anything else?"

"Nope! Let's eat!"

The weekend was full. Katie got her ice cream treat, along with Matthew and Carrie who shared their usual hot fudge sundae. Carrie got a few frames finished and listed on the Buy and Sell site that was the source of almost all her business.

Her most common set was a group of gold-painted frames with a little bit of black showing under the gold, giving an antique look to the collection of different sizes and shapes of empty frames. Now she was getting more creative, and with good results. But the finished product always depended on what she could find at the thrift store and the mis-tinted paint section of the hardware store.

This weekend's project was a very masculine-looking set of wood frames. She and Matthew sanded down and varnished them, then she inserted a piece of an old corduroy suit jacket big enough to fill the frame into each one. The finished set was an intriguing mix of textures that she was especially proud of, and she set the price at $100, with fingers crossed that it would actually sell for that much.

On Sunday afternoon, Carrie said something the kids had been waiting to hear since Christmas, "Let's go skating!"

"YAY!" Katie shouted with her usual enthusiasm.

Carrie was relieved that their skates still fit, and for an hour she forgot everything except having fun with her kids. None of them were very good, but they could mostly stay on their feet. The dance music pumping through the speakers at the arena somehow helped too.

That night Carrie lay in bed listening to Katie's even breathing as she slept, wishing for the feeling of peace that used to envelop her at night. One year ago, she had been living in terror of her then-husband Don and trying to squirrel away enough cash to escape. After she and the kids moved out, Carrie used to say a little prayer of gratitude each night when they went to sleep knowing nothing could disturb them. Now, nightmares and worries threatened to destroy that peace for her. She was still grateful for their new life, but wondered if she would ever win the battles that happened in her mind.

CHAPTER 2

Monday morning, she walked home from dropping Katie at preschool with a plastic bag for collecting bottles and cans for recycling in her hand. It had been a big moment for her when she no longer needed the spare change to make ends meet. Now Matthew and Katie got the cash after every visit to the recycling center. It was still a novelty for them to have spending money.

Back at home Carrie responded by email to someone who wanted to see the wooden frames that night, and then took stock of what she had to work with. One of her biggest challenges was finding enough low cost frames to work with. She was a regular at all the thrift stores in the area, but that didn't always work out. Fortunately, they were heading into yard sale season which was always a good source for frames and interesting fabrics to fill the frames.

She decided to group the last of her three small frames together. There was a pretty floral scarf that was big enough to divide and put into all three frames, and a shabby chic white paint finish would set them off nicely. Making sure a timer was set so she wouldn't be late picking up the kids from preschool, she got to work at the kitchen table. With a fine sandpaper she started by creating a perfect surface for priming and painting.

The timer shocked her out of her priming. It still amazed her how fast time could pass when she was focused. It was the same with her studying. The experiences were a sharp contrast to years past when the days dragged by painfully slowly without purpose or hope.

Today was the first day she would be taking care of Angela along with Magnus and Katie after preschool. When Magnus' mom Kara had asked Carrie if she could provide after-school care for him and his older brothers last summer, it was the opportunity Carrie was waiting for. Because of that income, she escaped from life with Don and gave herself and the kids freedom from his constant anger and verbal abuse.

A few months later, Kara introduced her to Angela's mom. Jenny was undergoing cancer treatments at the time, and with Kara's care as a Physician's Assistant and Carrie's support doing her housecleaning, she was now doing much better and was back to work full-time as a financial planner.

Beginning today, Carrie would watch Angela until just before three, when Jenny's brother-in-law Jonathan would pick her up until Jenny was done with her clients for the day. Three was when Kara's twin twelve-year-old boys Justin and Calvin walked home with Matthew and stayed until Kara finished work. Justin and Calvin weren't bad kids, they were just impulsive, rambunctious boys—too much for timid Angela.

As she walked home with the three preschoolers, Carrie couldn't help but smile at how different they were. Angela was the opposite of Katie. She was quiet, insecure, and very tentative about everything she did. Her mom's illness had affected her quite deeply, even though she was surrounded by loving parents and an uncle who doted on her. Carrie had seen Angela begin to gain some confidence, but she didn't want to ask too much of her. Fortunately Jonathan had a flexible work schedule, and he could watch Angela from three on.

Magnus was also quieter than Katie, but Carrie had already seen that the three children created a dynamic that worked well. Although Katie initiated almost everything they did, her enthusiasm helped to bring the other two out of their shells. And when Katie just had to burst out in song, do a dance, or play gymnastics with her teddy bears, Magnus and Angela would continue playing quietly together until Katie had gotten out enough wiggles to join them again.

After feeding the kids lunch, Carrie let them watch a DVD for half an hour. She still didn't have cable TV, so they were limited to whatever DVDs they could borrow from the library each week. At least now that she wasn't trying to study in every spare minute she could do more things with the kids, and the TV was finally spending more of the day off.

Just before three the doorbell rang. Carrie tried to ignore the little tingle she felt in her stomach at the thought of seeing Jonathan. He had also remained single by choice after suffering a devasting betrayal when his fiancé was killed in a car accident with another man. Although there were moments when Carrie found herself thinking about him as more than a friend, she did her best to ignore those. One screwed up marriage was enough for her, and she needed to focus on her own future with her kids.

Opening the door she had just a moment to get lost in Jonathan's eyes before Katie threw herself at him. Jonathan was taller than Carrie, with clear blue eyes, wavy blond hair, and a heart of pure gold. After running a very successful business in Singapore for years, he had given it all up to move back home when his sister-in-law Jenny was diagnosed with cancer. He was 100% committed to his extended family, which made him even better-looking.

Katie's energetic "Uncle Johnny!!!" interrupted their gaze, and he bent down to give her a big hug. As usual Katie had fully embraced the newest addition to her 'family' with great enthusiasm, and Jonathan didn't seem to mind.

"Hello there! What have you been up to?" When Katie let go of him, he turned to Angela who had quietly walked up after Katie and he put a gentle hand on her head and smiled at her.

Katie launched into a description of everything the three kids had done since getting home from school. Jonathan listened to her while Carrie gave Angela her shoes and coat to put on and handed Jonathan her little blue cupcake-shaped backpack. When Katie paused for a breath he took the chance to say good-bye to them before moving back out the door with Angela. He paused for a moment to turn back and look at Carrie. "Thanks for having Angela! I'll see you tomorrow then."

Carrie nodded and smiled before closing the door behind them. He really was an almost-perfect guy and she hoped that one day he'd find someone he could start his own family with.

There were just a few minutes to get a snack ready for the kids before Matthew came home followed by Justin and Calvin. As usual they were starving, and they tore into the apples, crackers, and peanut butter that Carrie had made before heading outside. Time spent at the big field and park across the street was crucial for helping the boys burn off steam and for keeping the time they were all in the townhouse to a minimum.

CHAPTER 3

The next morning Carrie put the $90 from her successful sale the night before into her purse before walking Katie to preschool. She tried to deposit cash as often as possible so she could see her grad school savings account continue to grow. At this point she felt confident she'd have enough saved for the first year. It was the second year that had her concerned. And covering her living expenses. And any surprises that might come up. And...so many things. She wondered if other women constantly worried too. If they did, they weren't talking about it.

After Katie joined her friends at school, Carrie and Jenny walked together back to Jenny's house. Jenny was a completely different woman from the one Carrie had first met last fall. At the time, she had just moved, her husband was traveling for work, and she was going through cancer treatments. When her housekeeper quit on her, both her life and her home were in chaos.

Carrie had done more than just clean up and pick up Angela from preschool. She had restored Jenny's confidence in others, encouraged her to focus on the future and the things she had control over, and helped her little family fully settle into their new home.

Now Jenny had a clean bill of health and was back to her full-time job as a financial planner. The year before, Jenny was the first person Carrie opened up to about her financial struggles and her deep fears about her ability to manage money and take care of her kids. With Jenny's guidance she made the decision to spend her cash windfall on getting her degree, rather than paying off the debts she had been saddled with from her ex-husband.

The two women chatted as they walked, enjoying the easy comfort of a relationship where each had seen some dark points in the other's life and still accepted her fully. All of Jenny's paying clients were high net worth individuals who were focused on wealth management rather than daily financial struggles, and her time with Carrie was a welcome break from the types of issues they faced.

As Carrie's business continued to grow, Jenny's coaching had shifted from basic budgeting and financial planning to tax planning and looking to the future. Carrie was probably the only person excited to claim all her earnings as it would help her begin to establish an income history. She knew she didn't want to live in her tiny two-bedroom townhouse forever, but it was only recently that she had allowed herself to start dreaming about buying her own home.

Carrie cleaned house for Jenny on Tuesdays and Thursdays while their kids were at preschool together. She often joked that it was like being at home—Jenny was the adult version of a Katie-tornado—and the condition of the house never surprised her. Jenny relied on Carrie's level-headedness and ability to put a messy house back together, and couldn't imagine what she had done before Carrie.

They sat at the table first for their routine chat—with tea for Jenny and coffee for Carrie—before Jenny moved to her office for her first online consultation of the day, and Carrie got to work putting Jenny's house back together. While Jenny insisted on paying Carrie $50/morning for her work, both ladies felt they were getting a far better deal than just money.

By Friday, the last of the frames Carrie had at the beginning of the week were either finished and for sale, or already sold. Now she needed to add to her stock as soon as possible or she'd lose that source of income—another thing to worry about. Although she was used to a stressful life, this worrying about everything was new to her. It was like her brain couldn't accept that things were going OK and had decided something terrible was always just around the corner. She didn't know what to do about it. Telling people how much she worried about everything when her life was going so well would be embarrassing.

Her thoughts were interrupted by her phone ringing. It was Maria, her friend Lisa's mom. Carrie enjoyed these two women who were creating a new life together after years apart. But she just couldn't bring herself to answer the phone when she was feeling so miserable.

An hour later Carrie was feeling slightly more capable so she listened to the voicemail from Maria, asking if she could create a frame for the wall in her new bedroom. She texted back that she could come with the kids anytime on Saturday, but it would be hard to do anything without frames to work with. She'd have to do a round of the thrift stores after the visit.

Lisa was a go-getter in her early twenties who had put her own goals on hold long enough to move her mom in with her when her dad had suddenly died. As the daughter of a mom with a disability, Carrie understood how challenging Lisa sometimes found it to help with Maria who had rheumatoid arthritis. And as the ex-wife of a man who had been abusive, Carrie also understood many of Maria's challenges in the aftermath of her own marriage to an abusive man.

The kids only vaguely remembered visiting with the two ladies in January, but they were always happy to go somewhere new. After her soccer game Katie insisted on first going home to change into different clothes. She really went all out for the occasion, layering colorful shirts and putting a rainbow tutu on over her jeans. In his own way, Matthew dressed up too, putting on his favorite button-up dress shirt with his nicest pair of dark jeans.

Carrie wished she had the money to take the kids shopping for nicer clothes. They still relied on whatever they could find in the thrift stores, and often pickings were slim. She had moments when she was tempted to just let loose and spend her savings on her kids, but then reality and fear would kick in. Finishing grad school and starting a practice as a counseling psychologist was the key to a better future for her and her kids, and she needed to stay focused on the big picture. There was no way of knowing what might happen next, and she needed to be smart with her money.

CHAPTER 4

Carrie and the kids were impressed when they pulled up to Lisa's new house. It wasn't that far away from their own, but the neighborhood was upscale, with large houses, professional landscaping, and fancy cars in every driveway.

Lisa's house was set further back from the road than the other houses on the street. In the driveway was an older model sedan—the only sign that the people living there might be different from their neighbors.

The freshly painted cream siding of the two-story house contrasted nicely with the green trim and the bright red door was very welcoming. On either side of the walkway were large pots filled with red and yellow flowers, and Carrie could see tulips starting to pop up in the flower beds underneath shrubs along the edges of the yard.

They went inside and Maria immediately turned to the kids. "Hello hello! Come on in and have a snack. Which kind of cookies do you like?" In less than a minute the three of them were at the table chatting and Lisa offered Carrie a tour of her house. She was so proud of what she had accomplished in fixing up the place. Carrie could only try to imagine what a disaster it had been when she bought it in

March. There was a quiet humility about Lisa that made it easy to just be happy for her and the new life she was building.

Maria's bedroom was bright and unique with her bed up against an orange feature wall and across from a large window letting in the late morning sun. Carrie was delighted with the accessible bathroom that they had installed. Because her own mom was in a wheelchair she understood how important the right bathroom would be to Maria as her illness progressed. Lisa admitted that the new bathroom gave Maria a level of independence she hadn't had before, and Maria's confidence was growing.

The biggest surprises of the tour were the huge frames Lisa had uncovered in her shed, and now had stacked in the garage waiting for Carrie. The largest one was at least three feet by two feet. Lisa wanted to give them to her for free, but Carrie insisted on exchanging them for a redone frame for Maria's room. Already she was itching to get her hands on them and create something that reflected Maria's fresh start with her daughter.

They joined Maria and the kids at the table, where Carrie gratefully accepted a coffee. The conversation turned to the changes all the ladies had undergone. Maria used the word transformations, which gave Carrie a chance to force her mind away from the memories of last night's nightmare that kept churning in her mind, and onto the two women in front of her.

With a cleansing breath, Carrie continued Maria's thought, "Transformations... I like that. Transformations. As women, we're never just one thing, are we? Or, if we are one thing for a time, it transforms into something new or extra. What about you Maria? What's your transformation?"

Lisa stopped her mom from answering and with a huge smile told Carrie about Maria's transformation from a fearful quiet woman to an outgoing people person who was constantly making new friends.

Carrie would have liked to keep chatting but the kids were getting fidgety and she decided it was time to leave. Just then the door to the basement suite opened and a lady came in who looked vaguely familiar. Matthew spoke up, "Hey, you're Becky's mom!"

He had talked a bit to Carrie about Becky and how some of the kids at school were mean to her because of her special needs. When he told the mom that he knew her daughter, her face lit up.

She introduced herself as Carla and reached out to shake Carrie's hand. "Nice to meet you!" She turned to Matthew, "And thanks for knowing Becky's name. Most kids just try to ignore her."

"She's alright," Matthew responded, suddenly shy. "I try to say hi to her during class. I think she tries to say hi back."

"She probably does," Carla assured him, "She really likes being around other kids, and she's pretty good at noticing the friendly ones. If she makes eye contact with you, that's one way she says hello."

"Cool!" Matthew responded, "I'll say hi again this week then."

Carrie and the kids headed out after thanking Lisa again for the frames, and both ladies for the nice visit. She would keep in contact with the two of them. It was always good to spend time with people who didn't let their past get in the way of their future. She needed that right now.

During the next few weeks, Carrie started to accept that the nightmares were a part of her life now. They didn't come every night, but when they did, they always felt as real and heart-crushing as the first one. For someone used to tackling problems head-on, she felt completely helpless to do anything about them. But getting help seemed just as futile. She worried that saying the things out loud that her mind came up with in the middle of the night was a sign that she didn't have a good relationship with her kids. Why else would she dream about them leaving her?

It took Carrie a few weeks to find just the right fabric to frame for Maria's room. She brought a few different pieces when she returned, but Maria chose Carrie's favorite one—a brilliant cream colored glossy frame around a silk scarf with swirls of red and orange. Lisa fell in love with one of the others—a shabby chic frame with a lighter colored scarf that Carrie had gathered at one corner to create a textured finish before framing it.

She had already sold four of the other large frames on the Buy and Sell site for $150 each and when Lisa found out, she insisted on paying the same for hers. Carrie still had two more large frames at home to sell and she had added to her stock after finding some good yard sales. It boggled her mind a bit that she had made almost $1000 in May, which went a long way towards her savings goal. Looking back, it would have been wise to shift to finishing picture frames earlier rather than spending so much time on refinishing furniture, which didn't have the same potential. Oh well, at least now she was onto something that worked—and worked really well!

After the ladies had admired the frames, Carrie joined them at the table for a coffee while the kids explored the backyard. There was a new feeling to the place, something she couldn't quite put her finger on. It turned out Lisa had made some big changes the same day she had visited for the first time.

Now, Carla, her husband Chris, and Becky were their new basement suite tenants, and they had hired Maria to watch Becky every day after school while Carla was at work. Maria practically glowed when she talked about it. "It makes the days go by so much quicker to have Becky here in the afternoons, and I'm finding it easier to understand her. And getting paid for it is just a bonus! It's the first time I've earned my own money since before Lisa was born!"

Lisa was also renting out one of her bedrooms on Airbnb and Carrie was intrigued to hear that it was working out really well. What a great use of a big house! A short while later they all said their good-byes and promised to keep in touch. Carrie went home with a light and happy heart. That night she got a text from Lisa inviting her and the kids to a housewarming party at the end of June. She immediately replied back that they'd love to come.

CHAPTER 5

Despite all the good things happening to her, most of the time Carrie felt like worrying and anxiety were a permanent part of her life and she needed to just accept it. In the past, she'd worried about specific things—like whether she'd get into university, and how to make ends meet as a student when the student loans ran out before the semester ended. But now it seemed like every thought was a worry disguised as a thought. She still worried about specific things like money and whether she was making the right choices as a parent, but there was also this constant lingering feeling that something bad might happen at any moment. It was exhausting, and discouraging, and she didn't know if it would ever get easier.

She wished she could be more like Katie, who would come to Carrie with a problem, climb in her lap for a cuddle, and then be able to hop down and go about her day in total confidence that everything would be fine.

One of the more immediate worries bugging Carrie was Kara's boys and the upcoming summer holidays. When she began watching them just before school started last summer it was tricky keeping them busy all day, but it had been temporary until school started. After that, she just watched them after school, which was manageable.

Now, she wasn't sure she could handle all the kids every day for the summer and it was starting to overwhelm her. She didn't want to lose the income for watching them, but the boys were older, bigger, and busier than they were last year. The logical part of her kept insisting that she could figure it out, but the anxiety about it all was much stronger. Finally, she texted Kara:

Got time for a coffee? I'd love to chat!

Kara replied that she had a break between patients from 11-11:30 the next day, so they planned to meet up at the little café beside the clinic Kara worked at.

That night the nightmare escalated. In it Don was still taking away the kids, but at the last minute he shoved her hard in the chest, and she felt herself falling backwards into terrifying blackness. She woke up shaking so much she couldn't get up. She lay there with tears of fear and frustration pouring down her face while she sobbed silently.

The next day she worked half-heartedly on the frames until it was time to meet Kara for coffee. She had just enough time to order a latte and grab a table in the corner of the café before Kara came in. Once she had her coffee Kara joined her.

"Hey girl!" She leaned over and gave Carrie a side hug before sitting down beside her. "I hate to cut out all the small talk, but I only have a little bit of time. What's up?"

Carrie dragged her wooden stir stick through the foamed milk on the top of her latte for a few seconds before starting. "I wanted to have a little chat about me watching the boys over the summer. I'd like to help you out in any way I can, but to be totally honest, I'm not sure if I can cope with the boys all summer. I've been trying to convince myself it'll be fine, but I'm not so sure." She paused and looked at Kara with a sad smile. "They're a lot bigger and busier than they were last year, and my house feels like it's shrunk."

Kara leaned back in her chair and looked up at the ceiling. "You're right. Ken's been trying to talk about what to do for the summer and I've been avoiding it. This is the first summer we'll both be working full-time and I'm having a hard time with it all."

Carrie suddenly realized she wasn't the only one struggling with life. She put her hand on Kara's arm, "What's really going on?" She was surprised to see tears pooling in Kara's eyes. Kara was always the calm, level-headed one. Carrie didn't remember her ever being emotional.

After looking up again and blinking her eyes rapidly Kara turned to Carrie. "The summers have always been so fun for me. Lots of sleeping in, no schedule, doing what we wanted when we wanted without worrying about school, or work, or anything like that. I love my job—you know that! But losing the summer with my boys is just devastating!"

"Wow. Kara, I'm so sorry, I never thought about how this would feel from your end. I guess it's almost like that moment when your kids go to preschool for the first time and you know you'll never have those special toddler times again."

"That's exactly what it's like! Although, just finally saying it out loud makes it hurt a little less. I've been trying to ignore thinking about it, but deep inside I've really been stirred up about it all. So…what do we do?"

Carrie found herself laughing, in spite of her own dark mood. "I have no idea! But you're right, talking about it makes it feel like a smaller problem already. Why don't I look around for some things near us that our boys can do during the summer, and maybe you can ask some people at work who have kids what they're doing for the summer?"

"Yep, that's a good start. I can do that. Oh, and Ken's parents are coming for a visit the first two weeks in August, so for sure during that time the boys will be home with their grandparents."

"That's perfect! Two weeks down, six to go! Do your parents want the kids at all during the summer?"

"I'll ask them. This is the second summer with Kevin in the group home, so maybe they're feeling up to having some hyper kids around for a week." Kara's brother was severely autistic, and her parents had focused almost all their energy over the years on his care until they finally found the right group home for him. Now he was happily settled, and her parents had been taking time to do things they hadn't been able to before, like go on vacation and fix up their house.

"OK. I think we have the start of a plan then. The Boys' Club that Matthew goes to has a couple campouts planned, and there's a Vacation Bible School at the church for a week near the end of July that Magnus and Katie can go to."

"What's Jenny doing with Angela?" Kara wondered. With Max's job taking him out of town frequently, Jenny had to plan ahead for the times she worked.

"She's going to her parents for the month of July and taking Angela with her. She'll still be able to keep all her clients with her virtual appointments, and her parents will be there to watch Angela when she's working."

"And if she needs you for the first two weeks in August, my boys will be away, so that might work out." Kara took a very realistic view of her boys and understood that some quieter kids like Angela found the twins quite intimidating.

Carrie admired her friend for the matter-of-fact way she approached being the mom of three boys, and how she had such good relationships with each of them. "I'll let Jenny know about August, thanks. Although I think with Angela being away for a whole month, Jonathan might want her all to himself when she comes back!"

"How's it working out to have him pick her up every day?"

"Good! He's such a decent guy, and he always has time to have a little visit with Katie before he leaves. She adores him almost as much as Angela does!"

"And what about you?"

"What?" Carrie pretended to not know what Kara was talking about.

"Every time I see you and Jonathan in the same area I can practically see the sparks flying between the two of you! When are you going to do something about it?"

"I'm not going to do anything about it! I don't know, maybe grad school will help me sort out the baggage I still have from being married to Don. But, in the meantime, Jonathan deserves someone who can be totally committed to him and is ready to move forward." Carrie ignored the little voice in her head that wanted to tell Kara about the nightmares and anxiety—Kara clearly had her own issues to deal with.

"Why can't that be you Carrie? You're so amazing, you've got this great ability to understand people and connect with them, I can tell that Jonathan is totally into you, *and* he adores your kids! Why would you deny having him in your life?"

"I'm pretty sure your rose-colored glasses are impairing your vision!" Carrie teased, trying to lighten the conversation. She refused to think about being in a relationship. With two kids, a business, grad school, and starting a counseling practice she really didn't have the time or energy for a relationship. Not to mention the dark hole she was struggling to avoid falling into. She'd just have to keep telling herself that until she could ignore the tug in her heart and the tickle in her stomach every time she was near Jonathan.

Once Kara had hurried back to work, Carrie drove home before walking to preschool to pick up the kids. On the way back with three kids in tow she thought over what Kara had said about losing her summer with her boys. She felt a bit the same way about Katie starting kindergarten in the fall.

The school offered full day kindergarten, and Carrie had signed

Katie up without a thought. But now that the start date was coming quickly, she felt like she was losing a little piece of her daughter. Sure, she'd keep busy with school and work during the day, but Katie brought a bright spark to every room that she was in, and Carrie knew she'd miss her desperately when she was at school. In that way her nightmare was coming true—her daughter would be out of reach every day.

CHAPTER 6

The middle of June brought good news and bad news about grad school. *Why does it always have to be both together?* Carrie wondered. It seemed like she deserved lots of good news and no bad news for once, but that's not how things were playing out.

The good news was that she had received an $800 bursary, and she was guaranteed it again next year. The bad news was that she didn't receive the $2,000 scholarship she had applied for. It was disappointing. Who could possibly need that scholarship more than her?

She tried to think positively. With the bursary, her picture frame sales, babysitting, and housecleaning for Jenny, her grad school account was at $9,700. She now had enough money to pay cash for her first year of tuition and she could start saving to cover her monthly expenses. In a perfect world she would feel happy about where she was, but in her world, she was just worried about what bad thing might happen next.

The week of Lisa's housewarming party Carrie was surprised to get a text from Jonathan:

Any chance you're free for coffee tomorrow when the kids are at preschool? I wanted to chat with you about something.

She tried not to read anything into it. Being one-on-one with Jonathan wasn't entirely new, but it didn't happen very often. He was probably planning another surprise for Jenny and wanted her help. At Christmas he had paid for Jenny's parents to fly in to surprise her for the holidays. Carrie thought it was one of the sweetest things she had ever heard of a guy doing, and that visit had been the key to Jenny's recovery.

They agreed to meet at 9:30 the next day, after the kids were dropped off. She didn't say anything about it to Jenny when she was cleaning, in case it was some sort of surprise.

That afternoon the kids were nearly impossible to manage. Matthew was out of sorts because his guitar lesson was cancelled, but Carrie knew the end of the school year tended to bring out the worst in kids anyways—they were wound up and ready for a break. Put five kids all together in a small space and the tension created bickering, complaining, and even an all-out fight between Justin and Calvin that led to Matthew's prized LEGO collection being crushed by flying legs and arms. She surprised herself and all of the kids by hollering, "ENOUGH!" Carrie never yelled at the kids, and everyone turned to her, shocked.

In her small place Carrie barely even had room to separate the twins and she ended up with one in the kitchen, one on the stairs, and Magnus and Katie confined to Katie and Carrie's bedroom away from everyone while she worked to help Matthew calm down. He almost never lost his temper, but the destruction of his things in his own space was more than he could handle.

Carrie sent a quick text to Kara to let her know what had happened so that she wouldn't have to talk about it in front of the kids, or pull Kara to the side to tell her. She hated it when parents shut kids away so they could complain about one thing or another and tried to never do it herself.

After chatting with each of the twins and deciding that they were now both calm and remorseful, she handed them back their Nintendo Switch (which had almost been another casualty of their fight) and made Matthew some hot chocolate to drink in his room where he could have some space. She was more than grateful that Katie and Magnus played nicely while she tried to deal with everything. By the time Kara came everyone was calm and happy again and Carrie could breathe a sigh of relief.

Thursday evening was library time, when they returned their DVDs, chose different ones, and picked a few books and CDs. Carrie was grateful for the free entertainment they received courtesy of the library and picked up a brochure about their summer programs when they checked out.

CHAPTER 7

Jonathan had walked Angela to school in the morning, so after dropping off the kids Carrie and Jonathan walked together to the coffee shop. He insisted on paying for her mocha alongside his latte, and by the time they were sitting at the table Carrie had a repeat loop of *it's not a date… it's not a date* going through her brain.

She was almost surprised when he spoke, she'd been concentrating so hard on keeping her thoughts and feelings in check.

"I was wondering how you were doing," he started.

"Oh, I'm fine thanks. How about you?" She was glad he couldn't look in her mind and see the nightmare from last night that kept replaying itself.

"I think I'd be better if I knew what was bothering you. It's been obvious for a little while now that you're *not* OK. Can I help?"

His sincerity and care completely undid Carrie. Without any way of stopping herself she found tears running down her cheeks. Embarrassed she grabbed a napkin and tried to mop them up. Jonathan's gentle hand on her arm made her look up at him.

"Seriously Carrie, tell me what's up. Please."

Carrie just didn't have the willpower to hold it all in anymore, so she talked about the only thing she was willing to admit to. She told Jonathan about how worried she was about making ends meet right when she needed to focus on grad school. Occasionally she had to blot the tears that insisted on continuing to fall. She was grateful they were in a bit of a private corner and the coffee shop wasn't busy.

"Thanks for telling me. I'm guessing you haven't told anyone else, and you're still going around making everyone else feel great while you feel totally miserable. Am I a little right?"

She smiled through her tears. "Yeah, I guess so. I'd much prefer to talk with people about *their* challenges." Boy, he had no idea how much she preferred to *not* talk about her own problems, and how much she was holding back.

"Well for the record, I want to hear about what you're going through. So maybe in the future you could tell me?"

"Maybe." She didn't want to encourage him to focus on her, but at the same time it really did feel good to talk to him.

Jonathan was desperate to swoop in and rescue Carrie and the kids. He knew he needed to move slow with Carrie and let her figure this out but it was almost physically painful to sit back and wait for the right moment. Carrie was the most independent and capable woman he had ever met, but he could see through her abilities and tough shell, to the pain and baggage she still carried around from her abusive marriage.

"So, what happens after grad school?"

Carrie dried the last of her tears, and her eyes lit up. "Well, I'm hoping that my frame business is doing well enough that I can help others who need me, even if they can't afford to pay too much. I think maybe even doing something like Jenny does, where I can have remote sessions with people, no matter where they live. And it's a long way away, but if the clinic Kara's working at still doesn't have a regular psychologist then I'll apply for a part-time position there too. They have the odd person come in on a temporary basis, but that's not really ideal for people that need to learn to trust someone before they can start to be helped."

"Every time we have a conversation I'm more impressed with you."

He seemed about to say something else so Carrie quickly cut him off. "It was really good to talk about this. Thank you! But now I need to get back to the house and do some work. And I'm pretty sure you've got work too."

Jonathan offered to walk Carrie home, but she declined. She needed space from him, and some time to think. And anyways, he needed to focus on finding a woman who was ready for him, not Carrie. She didn't say that out loud, but she wanted to.

As she worked on frames Carrie thought about their conversation. Of everyone in her circle, it was Jonathan who clued in that she was having problems. It bothered her a bit that he was so tuned in to her, but she wrote it off as him seeing her every day when he picked up Angela. Never mind that Kara saw her everyday too and hadn't picked up on anything. *That was different*, she thought.

The rest of the day passed without incident. Calvin and Justin were clearly making an effort to control themselves and behave, and Carrie made sure to point out how much she appreciated it. They were good kids, just energetic and enthusiastic and she wouldn't hold that against them.

CHAPTER 8

When it was time to get ready to go to Lisa's housewarming party the next day, Matthew wore his other good button up shirt and took extra care on his hair. Carrie loved that her boy actually cared about dressing nice and looking good. Again she wished she had money to buy the type of clothes she knew he'd love.

As usual, Katie threw on an eclectic mix of clothes that somehow worked perfectly together even though the pieces on their own didn't look like they'd match anything. Carrie wore her best jeans and a bright pink wrap blouse that she had found at the thrift store. She had splurged at the drug store and bought some concealer so she could hide the circles under her eyes. It was warm enough that she set aside the boots she wore almost every day and put on her sandals instead.

She wasn't sure if Lisa drank, so instead of wine she'd picked up a cute basket of colorful potted flowers she could set on her deck from the hardware store to bring as a gift. Once they arrived, Matthew and Katie immediately went off with Becky to play, and Carrie pulled Carla away to meet Kara. She was surprised at first to see Kara there before remembering that it was actually Kara that had introduced her to Lisa the year before. Kara was like that, always knowing who to connect so they could help each other.

The three ladies compared experiences at the school their kids all went to, and their plans for the summer. Carrie was happy to hear that Maria would be looking after Becky for the summer, as long as her health held out. She suspected the silent special needs girl and the sensitive lady recovering from her own abusive marriage and sudden death of her husband last summer would be perfect for each other. Without knowing how she would manage, she found herself encouraging Carla to call her if she ever needed help with Becky.

Looking over at the three kids playing, it seemed like Matthew somehow understood Becky, even though she didn't talk to communicate. He had taken a sign language book out of the library after they had met Carla the first time, but even without signing it looked like he was interpreting between Becky and Katie.

Becky was short for her age, looking like a seven or eight year old, and not an eleven year old. Her thin, blond hair had wispy curls around her face and brushed her shoulders. Carla had explained that mentally she was about two or three, but it was hard to tell because she didn't communicate much. Moving into Lisa's basement suite had been really good for the little family. Matthew told Carrie that Becky was doing better at school and seemed happier. He only had music class with her but he was observant, especially with kids others tried to ignore because they were different.

Kara and her husband Ken could only stay for a little while, since they had to take the twins to a soccer game. They had left their boys home with a babysitter.

"The thing is, my older boys pack a *lot* of energy into their little selves," Kara explained to Carla. "So, we do a decent amount of our socializing without them!"

"I guess our experience is a little different. We used to only go places we could take Becky until we moved here. Maria's the first adult other than Chris and me that Becky's really taken to. I have to admit, it's kinda nice to go out on our own!"

Kara raised her glass to the other ladies, "Here's to kid-free outings!"

"I'll drink to that!" Carrie laughed.

After Ken and Kara left, Carla and Carrie moved out to the deck where they found two chairs and sat down. Carrie loved the view from Lisa's deck—everything was either green or colorful! There were bright potted flowers close to the house and a large grassy space with an unusual looking tree and a lilac at the back, before the yard dropped into a small ravine.

Carla said that sitting outside the walkout basement suite in the evenings was like therapy, and next week Chris would get to work building a lower deck and firepit in part of the large backyard. Carrie could just imagine a fire burning low while the adults relaxed and Becky played nearby. In addition to Chris, Carla, and Becky in the basement suite, Lisa and Maria lived upstairs along with Lisa's friend Amy who rented one of the rooms. Lisa rented the other bedroom out on Airbnb and Carla said there was almost always someone there.

As they chatted, Carla shared her story with Carrie. She and her husband had lost everything during the downturn, including their construction company. They were forced to leave the town where they had lived and move in with Chris' parents. But his dad couldn't cope with being around Becky and had gotten increasingly cruel to her and Carla. When Lisa learned of their situation she immediately offered them the basement suite at a reduced rate. That same day they moved their few possessions in and started to recover from all that had happened in the past year.

"That's a lot of loss to go through in one year. Not to mention moving and having to start over. How are you managing?"

"Better now that we live here. It was so hard when we were at my in-laws because I could see how it was impacting Becky and there was nothing I could do about it. Now that she's doing so much better I can start to recover myself. And with Maria around to help with Becky I've been able to get a job. It's just at a grocery store, but it's full-time. So that salary, along with Chris' work, is really making a difference."

Carla explained that Chris could do any construction work he came across, so most days he worked as a subcontractor. He had laid all the floors in Lisa's place just a few months ago.

"What do you want going forward?"

"It's funny, even though things went so badly for us, we both want to start another construction company. A lot of the work we did was small renovations for seniors, or additions for growing families. Lots of feel-good stuff where the finished product was truly needed and enjoyed. Chris did all the hands-on work, and I made sure everything ran smoothly. We loved it! It's good that I have this steady income now, but I miss being with Chris every day."

Carrie smiled wistfully. Jenny and Max, Kara and Ken, her parents, and now Carla and Chris. She loved hearing about couples that were so well matched, and loved being together. It always made her feel better about the world to know there were still marriages that worked.

Shortly after, two ladies came in with enough food to feed a village. Lisa explained that they were friends that ran a Central American food truck in the city. They all lined up for food, and Carrie enjoyed meeting some of the other people that had become a part of Lisa's life.

Lisa's story was a true come-from-behind tale. She put herself through college while working two jobs full-time until she had saved enough to buy this house. Now she was a bookkeeper for a large company downtown and made enough to support her mom and herself. Carrie hoped that she could do the same as Lisa one day.

It was late afternoon when things started winding down, and Carrie hadn't even had a chance to visit with Lisa. She wished she had a house big enough to be able to invite more people over at once, but decided to at least invite Lisa and Maria over for dinner next Saturday. Maybe one day she could also invite Carla, Chris, and Becky.

When it was time to leave, she couldn't find Katie. Matthew was on the couch with his Nintendo Switch, and Carla had taken Becky downstairs. Finally she found Katie in the front yard with Lisa, who was showing her all the different tulips that had been popping up in her flower beds.

"Mommy! Look at these flowers! They're like feathers on sticks!"

Carrie had to admit, the colorful tulips with feathered petals were some of the prettiest she had ever seen. She passed on the invitation for dinner, and their thanks for the nice day.

Lisa was almost glowing. "It's been so much fun having everyone over!"

Carrie gathered up her kids and headed home. The perfect time at Lisa's was just the thing to help her shrink the dark mood that had been hanging over her head for the past few weeks. Yes, she had some challenges coming up—again. But if Lisa could rise above her problems then so could she.

At the same time, Lisa, Maria, and Carla were all enjoying cups of tea after cleaning up from the party and talking about Carrie. Lisa shared what she knew with Carla. They were all impressed with the single mom who was putting herself through university while raising two kids and making everyone's life around her better. None of them knew about the dark secret that woke Carrie up at night in a panic, and how many of her days were clouded with fear and worry.

CHAPTER 9

Saturday morning Carrie got up early to work on frames, but had no motivation to do anything once she was downstairs. Instead, she opened up her budgeting spreadsheet. In September Magnus and Angela would be full-time kindergarteners so her income from child-care would drop. Doing after-school care for Kara's boys would help, but not enough. If she still did house cleaning for Jenny then she estimated her income from both to be about $1,000. So, just to make ends meet without any new expenses popping up she needed an extra $250 every month. Plus the $9,000 she needed for her second year of grad school!

When she was finishing her undergrad degree, her goal was to earn an extra $800 per month to go towards grad school, and most months she had succeeded. But now she needed an extra $1,000 per month to cover her shortfall *and* save enough for grad school the following year. It wasn't impossible, but it felt like it.

When she heard Matthew starting to get up, she closed her laptop and went to make her coffee. She wanted to protect him from money worries as much as possible. He had seen a lot of adult problems already in his ten short years and she knew he used to worry about money. Her new business had been good for both of them. It made her smile to think of how excited he still got every time she made a sale.

Once her coffee was ready she went to sit on the couch beside him. Instead of picking up his Nintendo Switch, he just cuddled into her and together they enjoyed their quiet time together.

The plan for the day involved going for a long walk and collecting cans and bottles for the kids to recycle for spending money, and then having the kids entertain themselves for a few hours while she worked on frames. She decided she'd also better try to connect with Kara and finish figuring out the summer. It was only one week before school was out, and they really needed to get their act together.

By the end of the day she had a few more things organized. For the first week in July, Carrie would watch Kara's boys every day from 9-5:30. They decided that Carrie would take all the kids to the pool every afternoon, which would help keep them busy. Kara found a day camp for the twins for the next two weeks so Carrie would just have all the kids for an hour in the morning and an hour and a half in the afternoon. The church nearby was offering a Vacation Bible School every morning during the first of those two weeks which Matthew, Katie, and Magnus would all go to.

It still left the last week in July and two weeks in August to figure out with Kara, but she was feeling much better about the summer. And Kara had suggested $650 per week for those three weeks of childcare, which gave Carrie a place to start with her budgeting.

Tuesday, as Carrie and Jenny walked together, Carrie talked about her upcoming money challenges. Jenny suggested that growing her frame business was a good strategy for addressing her shortfall.

"Starting your own business can be challenging and expensive, but you've built something out of nothing—almost literally! Your costs are ridiculously low because you're so careful to find bargains on all your frames and supplies, and you haven't spent a penny on marketing. What you've done is really impressive Carrie!"

"Really? It's strange, I just see it as something that came from desperation and worked out OK. But you're right, the business is already in a pretty good place. I just don't really know what to do next. I definitely want to see sales continue to increase."

They turned into Jenny's driveway, and continued talking as they went inside and upstairs to the kitchen.

"I think a website could be a logical next step. That way you can reach a much bigger audience. And listen, I know you've said 'no' to this idea before, but once you've got the website set up I really want to feature some of your pieces on the wall behind my desk. I know several of my clients who would kill for original work from an up-and-coming artist! Of course, there are other people who will love your work too, but I'd like to be part of showcasing your art. Because it really is art!"

Carrie smiled, "All right. *If* I get a website I'll let you display some pieces. But only if you promise me that you'll keep one as my gift to you for all you've done."

Jenny reached out her hand, "Deal!" They shook on it. "Have you thought at all about a business name?"

"Actually, I was just thinking about the word *Framed*. What do you think?"

"I love it! It doesn't limit you at all, but it does speak pretty clearly about what you're working with! So maybe do some research about starting a small business. Who knows, maybe there's even a grant or something available that you could use to build the website. Oh, look, I need to scoot or I'll be late for my first appointment. But just so you know Carrie, I admire you every single day for your determination. You are amazing!"

Carrie sat at the table for a minute after Jenny left. It was the same thing Jonathan had told her. Strange, even though she *was* proud of everything she was doing, and she knew she was making some good choices, she still felt that all that success was outside of who she really was. Deep inside it was hard to think about being an amazing person, let alone believe it. She didn't hate herself or anything, she just didn't think she was anything special. And even before starting her counseling psychology courses, she knew that was a problem. That and her growing obsession with worrying about everything.

CHAPTER 10

Carrie breathed a sigh of relief as she closed the door behind Kara and the boys. She had done it! She had survived a month of watching five kids every day, keeping them fed, getting them to and from day camps, vacation bible school, swimming, and trips to the park. Now, Kara's boys were excited to spend two weeks at home with their grandparents and Carrie was taking her own kids to see their grandparents for a week.

On top of all the childcare, Carrie had made some big moves with her business. She found a local organization that helped underprivileged women start their own businesses. Through it she met a twenty-something lady named Erin who was starting a website design business. She developed an entire website for Carrie, at no charge, in exchange for using the site in her portfolio.

For Carrie it was truly a win-win. She had a beautiful, easy-to-use website where she could upload pictures and descriptions of everything she had for sale, and her customers could make purchases, arrange shipping, and even request custom pieces without the back-and-forth of the Buy and Sell site. Plus, she could help another struggling woman get a start in business. Erin was excited to show potential clients what they could do with the help of her services.

The only expenses Carrie had were $325 for a year of web hosting, and a 1.5% transaction fee for sales processed through the site's payment system. Erin's design was so eye-catching that the first time she showed her portfolio to a potential client, they purchased one of the large frames Carrie had just listed!

Carrie also registered her business name, and gave Jenny two bright orange framed scarves to put on the wall behind her desk where her online consultation clients could see them. Now she needed to keep the content on the website fresh and changing and be careful to not double sell anything that she also had listed on the Buy and Sell site.

One of the hardest parts of the summer so far was finding time to keep doing frames. There weren't many things that she could do while the house was full of kids, and her most productive times—when she was home alone—were almost non-existent. Still, she sold a total of $425 worth of frames which, along with the babysitting money, meant she was starting to move towards paying for the second year of grad school. Making progress towards her goals helped ease some of her anxiety about finances. At least she could look at the facts—the money she was bringing in—and use that against the worrying.

But for now, she was going to try and relax with her two kids over their typical Friday night supper of pizza. Tomorrow she was having Chris, Carla, and Becky over for supper, and on Sunday morning she and the kids would head to her parent's house.

She'd asked Jenny's mom for the lasagna recipe she made last Christmas, and tossed a Caesar salad to go with it. In her tiny kitchen she needed to have supper ready and the cooking mess totally cleaned up before guests came, because six people at the table would leave them nearly touching the cupboards when they ate!

They had a nice dinner together, with Carrie, Chris and Carla trading stories of growing up in small towns. She could tell Carla was continuing to feel better about their situation, and the couple were already keeping an eye out for the chance to start their business again. Like Carrie, they were saving as much as possible for a time in the future when they'd pursue their dreams.

After supper Carrie set the kids up at the table with playdough while she made coffees for the adults and they moved to the living room. The couple talked with great excitement about some of the projects they had worked on in the past including turning something barely livable into the nicest house on the block. Chris admitted that he'd really like to flip houses—buy them on the cheap, fix them up, and sell them for a profit. It sounded like a great idea to Carrie!

When it was time to go she reminded them again to call her if they needed anything. The three kids had played really well together, and Becky was smiling from ear to ear. She had even put a dress on for their visit—something Carla said she rarely agreed to. Katie complimented Becky on her dress a few times, and Becky was loving the attention she got from both kids.

They waved goodbye until Chris' truck was out of sight, and then went in to get packed for going to their grandparents. Carrie's dad had collected lots of frames for her to work on, so she packed a box of tools, paints, and paint brushes, in the hopes of finding some quiet time to do some work on them.

CHAPTER 11

Carrie and the kids loved being at her parents. They lived just over an hour outside the city, in a ranch-style house that was surrounded by farmland. The kids had lots of room to run around and make as much noise as possible, and Carrie's dad had found bikes for them both at yard sales. The kids spent hours riding up and down the long driveway.

Carrie's mom was in a wheelchair from a car accident she'd been in when Carrie was ten years old. While she occasionally had days when the pain kept her in bed, for the most part she was able to enjoy having her grandkids around.

"Grandma! Grandpa! We're here!" Katie shouted before she was even out of the car. She ran towards her grandparents who were sitting in the shade of the oak tree out front. It was a perfect summer day—sunny but not too hot—and Carrie could feel herself relaxing already as she sat down on the grass beside her parents.

Later on they all went inside, and Carrie unpacked her supplies so she could start working on some frames the next morning. After seeing what Carrie did with the frames, her mom offered to help, and it wasn't long before Carrie practically had a production line going.

Her mom was happy there was something she could do for her daughter, and they spend many pleasant hours during that week working and talking about the kids and Carrie's future.

For the first time, Carrie found herself checking her phone while at her parents. Her circle of friends had grown so much since Christmas, and keeping in touch with everyone kept her phone buzzing.

Kara: *Just confirmed the boys are at my parents for the last week in August. Woohoo!!! U OK to have them for one week before that?*

Carrie: *You bet! How it going with Ken's parents there?*

Kara: *Bliss! They take the boys out every day and by the time I'm home from work the boys are tired and dinner's ready. Am thinking of hiding their keys on the last day so they can't leave!*

Jenny: *This is what happens when Jonathan hasn't seen Angela for a month and takes her out for the day...*

Carrie thought the picture of Angela asleep at the table beside her uneaten supper was adorable. Jonathan was sending selfies every day of him and Angela at every child-friendly activity in the city. It was cute how much he had missed his niece.

On Saturday the kids stayed home with Grandma while Carrie's dad took her around to all his favorite yard sale and flea market spots. They had a great time together, and she had to admit, her dad's haggling skills sure made her money go far. It was nice to check out things that Carrie just didn't see in the city. At one yard sale she was able to snap up six more large framed paintings that were about the size of the ones she had gotten from Lisa—all for $20. The young man selling them was just happy to have them gone. The paintings were truly terrible, but the frames had a lot of potential!

Carrie hadn't planned on doing any more frames before she drove home the next day, but her mom was quite keen to see what one of the big ones would look like, so she spent one more afternoon working on priming the largest of the bunch. With the hot dry weather it was ready for a coat of paint before supper time. At one of the yard sales that morning Carrie had found an old hippie style skirt that had a patchwork of different blue fabrics interspersed with little mirrors. She painted the frame a deep navy blue to go with the fabric.

The next morning she framed the large rectangle of fabric she cut from the skirt and they all admired the finished product. Carrie had to admit, it was one of her best ones yet. On a whim, she took it outside and propped it up against the big oak tree in the front yard. She took a few pictures from different angles then went back inside and her mom watched her list it on her website. She set the price at $195, figuring she could always lower it if there wasn't any interest.

Finally, it was time to pack up and head back home. Carrie would be watching Angela full-time all week, and she wanted the house to feel calm and organized before Monday morning. There was barely enough room in the car for everything once they added in all the frames and fabric Carrie had bought the day before. It felt good to have so much potential with her!

As they drove the quiet roads home, Carrie realized that while she was at her parents' she had been free of nightmares and almost entirely free of the daytime worries that usually plagued her. Knowing they weren't a guaranteed part of her days was a relief. At least she knew they didn't *have* to be stuck in her brain. But she was still trying to understand what was going on and why. If she could just figure that out, maybe all of this would end and she could go back to feeling happy and hopeful every day.

When she was feeling especially optimistic, Carrie dreamed of having enough money to buy a big, wheelchair accessible house so her parents could come live with her. She knew her mom sometimes felt quite isolated because she couldn't go anywhere without her dad's help, and not every place near them was wheelchair accessible. In the city she could be much more independent, and she would thrive if she could see her grandchildren every day. But that was a very big dream for another day.

When they were home and unpacking the car, Carrie's phone rang. It was Carla, sounding very hesitant.

"Hi Carrie, I'm so sorry to bother you when you're just getting home from vacation, but I need to ask a favor. No pressure, if it doesn't work you can totally say no and I'll understand. I know you've got a lot going on—"

Carrie interrupted, "Carla, it's OK! What do you need?"

"Maria's had a major flare up of her rheumatoid arthritis and she can barely get out of bed. She's in so much pain, it's just terrible. And she can't watch Becky. Is there any way you could watch her? Lisa doesn't know when Maria will be feeling better, but she said to at least plan for this week to start."

"Actually, that will work out perfectly! I don't have Kara's boys this week because they're at their grandparents, and the little girl I'm watching is very sweet. I think the kids will all get along well together."

Carrie could hear Carla let out a big sigh, "Oh, thank you so much! I could have cancelled work if I had to, but they're having a lot of staffing problems right now and it would have really left them in the lurch. Does it work if I drop her off at 8:30, and Chris picks her up at four? Oh, and I was paying Maria $300 per week, but whatever your rate is I'm happy to pay it."

"$300 is fine, and if Chris is running late or something it's no problem."

"No, that'll be just fine. He starts at five in the morning right now, so having to pick up Becky will help him not have too long of a day."

"Great! The kids and I will look forward to seeing Becky tomorrow then!"

Now Carrie had even more reason to get the car unpacked and the house organized. And she was glad she had a chance to help out Chris and Carla. She definitely had a soft spot for people who were down on their luck and trying to make a go of it.

After everything was put away and Carrie had a load of laundry going, she decided to take the kids to McDonald's for supper. They rarely went out to eat, but she just wanted some time to hang out with her kids and not have to cook or clean up afterwards. While she loved cooking in her parent's big kitchen, it had been a lot of work to cook for five, so a break was in order.

While Katie was playing in the play place, and Carrie and Matthew were enjoying ice cream cones, her phone buzzed. "Oh my goodness!"

"What? What Mom? Is everything OK?" Matthew immediately started to worry.

"OK? Matthew, everything's great! Look, someone just bought two of my frames for $275 *plus* shipping! Oh, wait, we need to get supplies!" She hadn't expected any sales so soon, and suddenly felt anxious to get the order shipped out as soon as possible.

"That's awesome Mom! Did the one you just did at Grandma and Grandpa's sell?"

"It sure did. Wow, that's pretty fast turnaround. Can you go and get Katie? We should head over to the office supply store before they close at eight."

Carrie was grateful she had set a decent price for shipping. She had to buy bubble wrap, clear tape, cardboard, and labels, and still pay to ship everything. Now she needed to figure out how to get things shipped, preferably without dragging four kids to the post office tomorrow!

After Katie was in bed it only took Carrie a short while online to find a courier that had reasonable prices, good customer reviews, and would pick up things at the house. With Matthew's help she carefully packed up the frames and added a hand written Thank You note. It took longer than she expected, but by 9:30 it was propped near the door ready to be picked up tomorrow morning.

Carrie fell into bed afterwards with one regret—she should have taken pictures of all the frames they did at her parents in front of their beautiful tree before she left. Even though she technically had a back yard, it was just a square of dead grass surrounded by a tall, warped brown fence—not a nice backdrop for pictures at all. The only reason they went back there was to put aside the cans and bottles they collected before returning them. Tomorrow she'd just have to take pictures using the worn off-white wall behind her couch as a backdrop so she could put more things up on the website.

That night the nightmare came back in full force, and for the first time Carrie actually woke up Katie with her crying. "It's OK Katie-girl, Mommy just bumped her head." She said the first thing that came to mind, and it seemed to appease Katie. Carrie waited until she could hear Katie breathing deeply before sneaking downstairs to her chair.

She kept Kleenex there now. It was easier than getting up to get toilet paper every night she sat there and cried. She was starting to think of herself as two different women. There was the woman who was haunted at night by dreams and who always seemed to feel anxious, and the other one who went through her days pretending she was fine. Her sole focus some days was hiding what was really going on from everyone. What kind of a counsellor would she be if she couldn't even manage her own feelings?

She started to wonder if she should even be taking counseling courses. How could she help other people if she was just pretending to be OK herself? It felt impossible to think of giving up her dream. It also felt impossible to think of helping other people when she was such a mess.

CHAPTER 12

Having her first order ready to go gave her a reason to get up the next morning. Carrie hoped that it would be the first of many, and she spent hours during the next few days putting all the new frames up on her website. It was a lot more work than just putting up a Buy and Sell post, but she knew the website looked much better with more images.

On Friday Carrie was relieved to hear that Maria was feeling better and could take Becky again next week. She had texted Maria and Lisa regularly through the week, knowing how hard it was when a family member was bedridden.

Overall the week had gone really well. Although she spent far more time in close contact with the kids than she usually did, she felt they had all learned how to play with each other, and the three kids had done really well with Becky.

The hardest part was trying to take care of some of Becky's unique needs. Carla had warned her that Becky, although toilet trained, would just stand near the bathroom when she needed to go, and then she'd need a little help with the process. But later on when she saw Becky near the bathroom she totally missed the cue, and

Becky had had an accident. She felt terrible, although Carla tried to assure her that it was a challenge even for those that knew Becky well.

It was also hard to tell what Becky wanted. Carrie didn't want to force her to do anything, but she also didn't want to leave her on the outside of anything the kids were doing either. She was more exhausted than usual after the week, and still needed to get groceries before they could eat supper.

Dragging herself and the kids through the grocery store she was surprised when Katie yelled, "Uncle Johnny!"

Carrie turned away from the fruits and vegetables to see Katie already giving Jonathan a big hug. He reached out and fist bumped Matthew before looking at Carrie and saying hello.

"What are you guys up to?"

"We have to get groceries now because Mommy had Becky all week and she said groceries is a job for less kids!"

They all smiled at Katie's rather accurate imitation of Carrie. "Have you had supper yet?" Jonathan asked.

Again Katie piped up, "Nope. Friday is pizza night so we'll have pizza when we go home. What's your favorite pizza Uncle Johnny?"

"Mine's BBQ chicken. What's yours?"

"It used to be cheese, but now I like meat pizza too. Wanna come over for meat pizza?"

Carrie smacked her palm to her forehead before turning to Katie to correct her. But Jonathan saw his opportunity and jumped at it.

"Well, I have to get my own groceries home first. So how about I order some pizzas to be delivered to your house and I'll meet you there?"

"YAY!" Katie cheered.

Jonathan smiled at both happy kids before looking at Carrie. "Looks like the kids don't mind my cooking. You alright if I join you?"

Carrie really didn't feel like she could say no, so she agreed. They both finished their shopping at the same time, and he promised to be back at her house before the pizzas came.

Back at home, Carrie looked around with dismay. Even though she had no interest in impressing Jonathan, she wished the house was a little cleaner. *That's what he gets for accepting Katie's invitation!* she decided.

Matthew helped by getting plates and cups out, and Jonathan arrived right alongside the pizza delivery lady. He paid and then came inside with two huge boxes.

"Are you expecting company?" Carrie laughed.

"It's a bit more pizza than I pictured," he admitted "so perhaps I'm bringing you breakfast too."

"Pizza for breakfast?"

"Sure bud," he answered Matthew. "It's the perfect breakfast food. What, not in this house?"

"We never have leftover pizza," Carrie admitted, "so we've never had it for breakfast!"

"Guess you'll get to try it out tomorrow!" Jonathan smiled.

Dinner was a lot more energetic with Jonathan there. He was able to keep up with Katie's chatter no problem, but he also managed to keep Matthew in the conversation. For the most part Carrie just enjoyed eating a pizza that hadn't been frozen first and having someone else to answer Katie's constant questions. Tonight, that was very welcome.

After supper Katie brought out Candyland and they stayed at the table playing until it was Katie's bedtime. When Carrie came down from tucking her in Matthew was showing Jonathan a game on his

Nintendo Switch. Carrie made hot chocolate for Matthew and decaf coffees for the adults. She sat in her armchair and curled up her feet under her while she savored her coffee.

"Mom? Mom? It's my bedtime." Carrie tried to pull herself out of her sleep to answer Matthew's soft voice and gentle touch on her arm. Opening her eyes, she saw Matthew in front of her and Jonathan on the couch, looking like he was trying not to laugh.

"Oh, shoot. Thanks bud! That's a little awkward. I hope you guys had a good visit!"

"We did Mom! It was fun. Jonathan would've played more but I said you'd want me to go to bed."

She reached out and gave Matthew a big hug, "You are such a fantastic kid! Thanks for being so responsible. You go get ready, I'll come up and say goodnight in a few minutes."

Matthew said thank you and goodnight to Jonathan before going upstairs. Once he was out of hearing range, Jonathan spoke up.

"That is the most surprising thing I've ever seen a kid do!"

"Yeah, he's definitely one of a kind! I honestly wish sometimes that he'd just relax a little bit more. He even does his homework without being told. But I am grateful for him and all of his goodness."

"I was going to ask if you wanted to watch a movie or something after the kids were in bed, but I have a feeling anyone who falls asleep before nine on a Friday night probably needs sleep more than a movie. Maybe another time."

"Maybe," Carrie replied. That answer was beginning to be a habit with her. "Thanks so much for bringing pizza and hanging out with us. The kids had a great evening—much better than they would have had with just me falling asleep on them!"

She got up and Jonathan followed. At the door he reached over and gave her the quickest kiss on the cheek before letting himself out and closing the door behind him. Carrie just stood there for a moment, her hand on the spot where he had kissed her. Finally, with a sigh she turned and made sure both doors were locked and the lights were out before heading upstairs to say goodnight to Matthew.

In her own bed on the floor, she fell asleep almost immediately and slept straight through until eight the next morning.

Jonathan let himself into his house with a smile still on his face. He couldn't have planned the evening better if he had tried. Even with Carrie falling asleep. One day he'd tell Katie how helpful she had been! He put his keys on the hall table and walked into the living room to turn on the TV. After an evening with two lively kids his own house was way too quiet. He left the lights off so he wouldn't see all the projects waiting to be finished. Tonight, his bright idea to buy a big house and flip it didn't seem so bright. He wished he was a few blocks away at a tiny little townhouse filled with love.

CHAPTER 13

Carrie allowed herself the luxury of lying in bed for a bit on Saturday morning before wandering downstairs to get coffee. Saying a quick good morning to Matthew, she checked over her numbers in her budget. It was amazing. She was definitely in a decent place, thanks to the sales from her website.

"Mom? Why are you just sitting there smiling?"

"Why? Don't I always stare out the window and smile?"

"No…Is it because Jonathan came over last night?"

She was shocked at his question, but hoped she could hide it. "Silly boy! Come here." She reached her arms around him and gave him a big hug. How was it that this kid was such an amazing person, considering where half his genetics had come from?

"I was actually just thinking about my budget, and it made me really happy. Guess what we're going to do today?"

"Go collect more cans and bottles?"

"Well, we can bring a bag along with us. But that's not it. We're going to go to the thrift stores to look for new school clothes for you and Katie, and then we're going to buy all new school supplies—whatever you want!"

Matthew pulled back from his mom's hug and looked at her face. "Really? I don't have to go to the needy kids center this year?" In the past, the only way Carrie could get school supplies for Matthew was to register at a charity that provided a set list of items for free. She had been very grateful for the help, but this year she had delayed registering in the hopes that she wouldn't need to.

"Nope. This year you get to pick your own supplies!"

"What's my budget?" Carrie reached up and ruffled his hair—just a little bit, because he really preferred to keep it tidy.

"There's no budget Matthew. We're going to get everything on your list, and a new backpack. I've carefully checked my finances and we are good to go!"

"Awesome! When can we leave?"

"As soon as we're ready, but I don't want to rush. We've got all day if we need it. Now, which kind of pizza do you want to have for breakfast?"

Carrie left him eating and went to give Katie a first wake-up call before hopping in the shower. It had been nice not to have to wake Katie up this summer. Another perk to babysitting in her own home. She couldn't imagine having to get her up and out the door early when it was supposed to be her holidays!

The day turned out to be one of the best of the summer. For the first time ever Carrie could take her kids to the store and say yes. They did pretty good at the thrift stores, finding some shirts and pants for both kids, and a few pairs of leggings for Katie. There weren't any decent shoes at either thrift store, so Carrie added them to the list of things to buy new. She also picked up a few more interesting picture frames and a cream cashmere sweater for herself that would be perfect on a cool fall day.

School supply shopping was crazy. Since Carrie had never been to buy supplies before, she had no idea the chaos that ensued. It was eleven by the time they got there, and it seemed like everyone was scrambling to get their supplies. They were only halfway through Matthew's list when Carrie pulled the two kids aside for a breather. Next year, she'd get this done before August!

Finally they had everything on Matthew's long list and Katie's little list, and the kids had each chosen new backpacks and lunch boxes. The only tricky time came when Katie realized she wouldn't be eating lunch at home once school started. Carrie explained that Katie would have lots of new friends to each lunch with, but she could tell Katie was unimpressed with this new change to her schedule.

"How about we have lunch at the food court to celebrate surviving school supply shopping?" Carrie suggested.

"YES, YES, YES!" shouted Katie at the same time as Matthew said, "Whoa, are you sure Mom?"

"Definitely," she said grinning at both kids, "Besides, soon we'll be back to boring sandwiches in those lunch boxes, so we should enjoy this!"

Just being in the mall was a novelty, since Carrie had always tried to avoid places where she'd be tempted to spend money. To be here now, *and* to know that she was OK to spend money on her kids hit her suddenly when she saw both of them staring at all the food options around them. Seriously, were there any other kids in the western hemisphere who hadn't been to a food court?

Before she could get emotional Carrie gave her head a shake and focused on getting the kids fed. Of course, they both went to the one place they recognized, but Carrie treated herself to something new and they all enjoyed their lunches.

Afterwards it was time to get new shoes for both kids. While they were looking, Matthew tapped Carrie on the arm.

"Mom, if I keep my indoor shoes instead of getting new ones, could I get my hair cut from the lady who does Justin and Calvin's?" His question totally threw Carrie. She had been cutting all of their hair for as long as she could remember, and thought she had gotten pretty good at it. It hadn't even occurred to her that Matthew might want a professional cut, but it should have, considering how careful he was with his hair.

"Bud, I think you've had your mom cutting your hair for long enough! How about you get new indoor shoes *and* a proper haircut?"

"Can I get a haircut too Mommy, pleeeeeease?"

Carrie looked at her two beautiful children, and realized for the first time that she wasn't exactly the best hairdresser. "You bet! I'll text Kara right now and ask for the number for their hairdresser." Kara often talked about her hairdresser who came to the house regularly to give the whole family haircuts.

After Carrie had paid for the shoes she felt her phone buzz. Kara had already sent the contact info. "Remind me to call when we get home," she said to Matthew.

Back at the house, they dumped their bags at the front door and Carrie collapsed in her armchair. Shopping was more tiring than watching kids! That evening she went through the shopping, clipping off tags, and taking all the clothes downstairs to be washed before the kids wore them. It was tempting to just throw away the receipts, but Jenny had coached her about the importance of always knowing what was going in and out of her account, even if the numbers weren't big or nice. Plus, she had used her credit card for a few purchases, and she wanted to pay it off right away.

Part of Carrie's legacy from her first marriage was a joint credit card balance that her ex left her with. Having to make a payment on it every month—even when it meant she had to cut back on other things like groceries—had left her with a fear of getting into debt. Jenny kept telling her that she was doing great with her finances and budgeting, but the echoes of her ex-husband telling her how terrible she was with money were still loud in her mind. If she wasn't trying to build up her credit in anticipation of one day qualifying for a mortgage, she would never use a credit card.

CHAPTER 14

Monday morning Carrie braced herself for one more busy summer week with five kids. Since Justin and Calvin were now following Matthew's lead in saving money from recycling cans and bottles, she planned some long walks in the different parks in their area. It would give the older kids something to do while Magnus and Katie inspected sticks along the way, and it was a good way to help clean up the environment. Carrie still couldn't understand how people could just drop something that was actually worth money, but as long as they did, her kids would have a small way to earn money.

In the afternoons they went swimming and then Carrie let them have screen time until Kara picked up her boys. It was all working out surprisingly well, until there was a knock on the door Wednesday morning. Carrie was trying to get the kids ready to go for another long walk, so she didn't hear the first knock. By the time Matthew answered the door, there was an impatient looking lady standing there.

"Is your mom here?" She stood there holding a clipboard and her face said they were a huge inconvenience to her day.

"Yes, that's me!" Carrie called out from the stairs where she was waiting for Magnus to tie his shoes. She was determined that he'd master it before kindergarten, and he had—if he had lots of time. Leaving him to continue, she stood up and went to the door. "Hi there, I'm Carrie."

"My name's Theresa Sanders, I'm the new housing manager. I believe you're overdue on your lease renewal. You were supposed to hand in an application by the end of July."

"I was? I'm sorry, I didn't realize that. Things have been really busy—"

"—*Mrs.* Bennet. That's no excuse. The purpose of this association is to provide subsidized housing, not act as your personal secretary."

Carrie had no idea what had turned this lady into a sourpuss! "No, of course not. What do I need to do?"

"Well, technically I could issue you an eviction notice immediately, since you're in violation of your lease agreement."

"MOMMY! Are mean men going to make us go away? Are we in trouble?" Katie had vivid recollections of the last time she had seen her dad when the bailiffs had come to evict him. A furious Don had dragged the two kids back to Carrie's in their pajamas, and in tears.

Carrie crouched down and put her hands on Katie's shoulders. "Honey, everything's going to be OK. This is different. But I need to talk to this lady without you interrupting. Do you understand?" Katie nodded reluctantly.

Standing up, Carrie squared her shoulders and looked the lady in the eye. "Is there a way to discuss this without little ears being affected? I'll take care of whatever needs doing."

The lady sniffed, and looked past Carrie into the townhouse. Her eyes scanned the group of kids all standing at the door. "Are you running a daycare?"

"No. These three boys are my friend's, and Matthew and Katie live here."

"Well, I'm sure you know that operating a business is not permitted. We have a lot of people trying to abuse the system Mrs. Bennet, and it's my job to catch them. All the information about renewing the lease is in the paperwork you received last year. I'll give you until Friday at four to submit it, and you'll need to pass an inspection too. Good-bye." With one last suspicious look at Carrie and all the kids, she turned and marched down the pathway.

As soon as Carrie closed the door all the kids started asking questions at once. "Stop! Guys, just hang on. I'm sure she's just having a bad day. Everything will be fine. But how about you all have screens for half an hour and then we'll go walking, OK?"

Everyone except Magnus was happy to take off their shoes and go back to their devices. With a sigh he started undoing the perfect bows he had just finished tying.

With a sinking feeling, Carrie went to the file folder in the kitchen where she kept her important papers. She had assumed this lease was just like the last house they had lived, where it just rolled into another year until she or the landlord gave a month's notice. It hadn't occurred to her that there might be different rules.

As she read over the agreement she had to fight to keep her panic down. Not only did it say she had to apply each year to stay *before* her move-in anniversary, but it also said she was not permitted to operate any business from the residence. If she did they could evict her immediately. What kind of crap was that? Were people just supposed to stay here in poverty and never have a chance to improve their finances? She was well and truly screwed. All that wicked lady had to do was ask her neighbors if she was watching kids regularly or selling anything out of her home.

She wanted to call her sister who was a lawyer on the coast and ask if there was anything she could do, but the answer was staring her straight in the face. With multiple violations to the lease agreement, it was only a matter of time before she was kicked out.

In the background she could hear kids starting to squabble. She had to get them out of here before anything happened. Quickly she sent a group text to all her local friends:

> *SOS!!! Wicked witch of the housing association just came by. I'm in big trouble and need a new place to rent. Like tomorrow. Or today.*

She pressed send before she was tempted to take it back. Forget hiding her troubles from everyone. This one affected her kids, and she needed help.

"OK everybody! Let's saddle up and blow this popsicle stand. Shoes on!" Forcing a smile on her face, she chose to pretend that everything was fine.

Ten minutes later they were all walking through the housing parking lot, bags in hand. Carrie could see the mean lady at another person's door, and the woman she was talking to was crying. *Horrible, horrible person! Did she really get off on terrifying people and threatening to take their housing away?*

She tried to focus on watching the kids and answering the million questions they fired at her while they were walking. But inside she could feel acid churning in her stomach and moving into her throat. What could she do? That lady probably wasn't going to cut her any slack, so she needed a plan right now.

With resignation, she decided she'd call her parents tonight when the kids were in bed. Moving home would be a lot better than being stranded with no place to live. There was no way she could find a place and move right away. She almost regretted sending in the bank draft for her tuition already. That was money she could have used for moving expenses. She'd have to check her budget as soon as possible. There was an emergency fund of about $1,300 in her checking account, plus some money saved for next year's tuition…. Nothing like one step forward two steps back!

Her phone buzzed a few times while they were walking, and she quickly looked to see encouraging messages popping up from everyone. She couldn't text back with five kids to watch, but it *was* nice to know people cared.

For the rest of the day Carrie had too much going on to deal with the housing situation, but that didn't stop her from worrying about everything that could possibly go wrong. And chastising herself for not paying attention to the small print on her lease agreement. It didn't matter that the rules were totally unfair, it was her fault for not being more careful.

When Kara arrived to pick up the boys Carrie promised to send out another text explaining everything. She didn't want to talk about it in front of the kids, but she'd have to figure out what to tell them soon. As soon as Kara left, Carrie sat down on the stairs and wrote the text:

> *So, stupid me didn't read my lease carefully. I was supposed to apply for permission to extend the lease one month before our move-in anniversary (August 15). AND the freaky housing lady asked if I was running a daycare and said operating a business out of the house was a violation that leads to eviction. Unfortunately I read the fine print after she left, and she's right.*
>
> *I think I'm going to have to move in with my parents. I have until Friday to apply for a renewal but there's no way to hide the fact that I'm running businesses out of my house. Feeling pretty devastated, and haven't told the kids yet. Or my parents… wish me luck!*

After hitting send, she set her phone on the floor and put her head in her hands. Two little arms wrapped around her. "Don't be sad Mommy!"

Looking up at Katie on the stairs behind her, Carrie felt her heart catch. Moving was really going to mess with Katie. Everything she knew was here, and she'd have to leave it all to start kindergarten in a strange school with no friends. She'd be devastated.

Carrie couldn't bring herself to tell the kids the bad news. "Thanks

Katie-girl! You always make me feel better! I guess we should go make supper." She got up and forced a smile for her daughter's sake. *Pretend you're fine until the kids are asleep, and then you can cry until morning.*

There was no way she could deal with this tonight. Besides, it wouldn't make any difference. Even if she found a place to rent, it wouldn't be until the beginning of September, or even October. What was she supposed to do in the meantime? Sleep in her car?

The next morning Carrie had just made her first cup of coffee when Kara arrived with the boys. At least without sleeping much there was less time for nightmares. But she was exhausted.

"Hey," Kara looked in at Matthew on the couch and then at Carrie who gave her friend a little shake of the head. *Please don't say anything.* She seemed to realize Matthew didn't know anything yet. "So, any news about anything?"

"No, nothing's changed since yesterday." Carrie had to fight to stop the tears from coming. That was the *last* thing she could let herself do right now! "We'll figure something out."

"Alright, I'll keep my eyes and ears open. Hang in there!"

"Thanks, have a good day at work!"

Kara smiled sadly at Carrie before leaving. Today would be a long day for both of them.

After she finished her coffee, Carrie forced herself to look online for places to rent. She had to try, even though every part of her just wanted to give up. But with little ears everywhere in the house there was no way to phone and ask about anything. She really should have told the kids last night that they'd be moving.

Just then her phone rang. Carrie looked down and saw it was Carla. For a moment she was tempted to ignore it—she just couldn't think of adding one more thing to her day.

"Hi Carla,"

"Hey Carrie, are you OK? I can't believe they'd treat you like that! But I may have a solution… I hope you don't mind that I told Chris what was going on. He's working on a job fixing up a house right near you that was trashed by the previous renters, and he told the landlord about you this morning. Can you pop over and take a look at it? Chris already told the landlord you'd be a fantastic tenant."

"Seriously? Oh, Carla, that would be great. But I've got Kara's boys here all day… Do you think I could go after 5:30?"

"Let me check with Chris and get back to you. I think the landlord has a day job, so maybe the evening would work better for him too."

"Of course, that's fine! But I'll have to bring the kids."

"I think it's a good idea to bring the kids so he can see how cute they are! I'll call you back as soon as I know anything."

It wasn't until the afternoon that Carla phoned back. "It's a go! He can meet you there at six tonight. Chris will be gone by then, but he's given you a really good reference. This guy is pretty worried about his house getting trashed again, so maybe the personal connection will help."

Carla gave Carrie the address. It was just a few blocks from their townhouse so they could walk there after Kara picked up the boys. She had just enough time to talk to Matthew and Katie before they had to leave. "So guys, there's a chance we might move to a different place! It's just nearby, and hopefully it's nicer than this place. I don't know much about it, but we're going to go check it out and I want you to be on your very best behavior when we get there, OK?"

"What? Now?" Matthew didn't like doing anything on short notice.

"Yeah, bud. I'm sorry it's such short notice but we need to see if this house might work for us."

"Is this because of that lady who came yesterday?"

"It is. So, maybe this is a sign that everything will work out."

Matthew looked like he wanted to say more, but Carrie stopped him, "We can chat about everything later, OK?" He nodded.

"Mommy! I want to chat about everything too! I have lots to say!"

"I'll bet you do Katie-girl. How about you chat while we're walking to the house. I'm all ears."

The house was about a ten minute walk away, but in a neighborhood they had never been to before. It was nicer than their townhouse complex, with a variety of bungalow style houses and a few bigger houses here and there. They passed a sign indicating a playground zone and Carrie promised the kids they'd check it out after they saw the house. She was already worried. By the looks of the neighborhood any house would be way out of her budget.

The front yard was nothing impressive, just a rectangle of dried grass with a pathway running through the center of it. But there was a driveway to the side, and the house was an adorable bungalow style. The front door was partly open, so Carrie knocked on the door and waited.

A man about Carrie's age came to the door. Just a little bit taller than Carrie, he had short dark hair and was wearing a white dress shirt and dark pants with a red tie loosened around his neck. He looked at Carrie and the kids without smiling.

"Hello!" she started, "I'm Carrie, and this is Matthew and Katie. We heard from Chris' wife that you might be looking for new tenants?"

"Yeah, I'm Jason. Come on in."

They followed him into the house, and Matthew and Katie started to take their shoes off.

"Oh, don't do that. It's too dirty in here for no shoes right now. But make sure you take them off later if you live here."

The inside was surprisingly spacious. It looked like the interior walls had been taken out at some point, and the living, dining, and kitchen areas were all open. There was light coming in from the large front and back windows, and Carrie could still smell fresh paint.

There was new laminate flooring laid everywhere except for the front entrance which had gray tile. The only thing missing was the trim around the floor and windows. They followed Jason into the kitchen where Carrie couldn't help dragging her finger along the brand new oven.

"Mom! Look! A dishwasher!" Matthew pointed.

"Can we have this place Mommy? Pleeease? I don't want to wash dishes anymore!" Katie begged.

"We'll see," Carrie responded absently.

She had to tear herself away from the kitchen window's view of a big, fenced backyard. The rest of the house didn't even matter. This place was perfect already. And there was easily enough room on the main level to set aside an area for doing frames. A big window in the dining area also looked into the backyard. Again, it wasn't much to look at, but there was a tree and a little shed, and a gate to a back alley. A door from the dining area led into a laundry room with a newer looking washer and dryer and another door to the backyard.

Upstairs there was a full bathroom, two medium size bedrooms, and one smaller bedroom that had just enough space for a bed and a dresser. Carrie wasn't an expert in home improvements, but it looked like the work Chris was doing to fix up the house was perfect. Even the transition of the laminate floors between the rooms was exact.

"There's only the one bathroom in the house, and the one bedroom is quite small but everything's top of the line here."

"Well, we're used to one bathroom already, and Katie and I share a bedroom right now so your place is looking pretty good! I guess the only thing is how much rent is, and maybe if you know how much utilities are every month?"

"Let's go downstairs. I have the paperwork on the counter."

As they were following him downstairs, Matthew asked the one thing that had been on his mind for years. "Are people allowed to have a dog here?"

Downstairs, Jason stopped and turned to Matthew. "I've had some pretty big problems in the past with dogs damaging the house. In fact, that's part of why I've had to put all new flooring in. And they weren't supposed to have a dog in here. Cost me a lot of money. No dogs, no pets."

Matthew's face fell. "Oh."

"So," Carrie stepped in, "How much is rent?"

"It's $1,250 per month and $1,000 damage deposit. What do you do for a living?"

Carrie hadn't thought about qualifying as a renter. Shoot, if he knew she was a grad student, or that she babysat to cover her expenses, he'd probably say no. "Oh, I have a business selling original art. It's called Framed. I have one regular corporate client locally, and I sell almost worldwide." It was a stretch, and although not dishonest, it didn't really feel honest either. She hoped the kids would keep quiet.

"Really? Do you have a website?"

"Of course, here…" Carrie took out her phone and pulled up the website. He put it into his phone and started scrolling through. Thank goodness she had a decent number of listings right now!

"These aren't bad. Who's your corporate client?"

"It's Eleanor Leung. Her company's called Design Right Interiors I think." Carrie hoped she remembered the name. She had only seen it once when Eleanor gave her a business card.

"Do you do custom orders?"

"Sometimes. Everything is repurposed so it can take a bit of time to find the right products."

"I'll have my PA call you. We need some things for the office."

"Great, thank you. Um, about the house…"

"Oh, right. You can move in as soon as Chris is done and the house is clean, probably next Thursday or Friday. I need the damage deposit and first month's rent right away, and postdated checks for rent going forward."

Carrie took a big breath and held it for a moment before exhaling. The rent was more than she had expected. If her sales continued to be good it shouldn't be a problem, but she didn't know for sure if she'd be OK. Maybe she shouldn't have spent so much money on school shopping.

Jason's voice changed when he saw her hesitation. "How about I show you the basement while you think it over? It's a very nice house, and I know you'll like it. The neighbors are great. I lived here for a year when I first came to the city so I can vouch for the neighborhood. And the school is really good." All of a sudden he was *trying* to get Carrie to rent the house.

They followed him downstairs, and the basement clinched the deal. It was fully finished, with a storage area in the furnace room where Carrie could keep her extra supplies, and a gas fireplace along one wall with a fully carpeted area that was begging for comfy seating.

"It does get a bit colder down here, but I put the fireplace in so it will stay really cozy. The carpets are new and everything's been repainted."

"It's perfect!" she exclaimed. "We'll take it, if you'll take us."

He reached out his hand and shook Carrie's hand. It seemed like he held it for a second too long, but she wasn't sure.

"Great! It's a really nice house, I'm sure you'll take good care of it."

Back upstairs, they used the kitchen counter to sign the lease. She wrote out checks for the damage deposit and rent and tried not to cringe as she imagined her savings disappearing. As soon as the kids were in bed tonight she needed to make sure to move the savings out of her grad school account and put them in her checking account with her emergency fund.

At the front door, Katie asked her mom, "Is this going to be our new house Mommy?"

Carrie took a deep breath and smiled, "Yes, it is Katie-girl. Aren't we lucky?"

Instead of answering, Katie turned to their new landlord and reached her arms up to him, with trademark Katie enthusiasm. He hesitated for a moment before bending down and awkwardly patting her on the shoulder. "Thank you for my new house! It's the bestest!"

He turned to Carrie and smiled, "I'll call you as soon as the house is ready."

They all said good-bye and walked out the door of their soon-to-be new house. Carrie looked around her, wondering what her new neighbors would be like. She was pretty sure anything was better than where they currently were. They had always put up with their noisy neighbors whose kids were constantly yelling and leaving their things strewn across both front yards. To have her own space with a fence on either side would be heavenly.

Matthew was quiet while they walked. Carrie appreciated that he must have lots of questions but was waiting until Katie was in bed. They turned down the street towards the playground. It looked like this was also where they could access the alley at the back of the house.

Suddenly, Katie darted out and Carrie just had time to grab her arm before she could run across the street. "Uncle Johnny!" she called.

Sure enough, coming out the door from a house across the street was Jonathan, carrying a toilet of all things. They crossed the street and he put down the toilet and met them on the sidewalk.

"Probably shouldn't hug me this time, Katie!" She looked at the toilet and made a face. "What are you all doing here?"

"We got a new house!" Matthew answered, "And it's got a big yard, and Mom will have her own bedroom, and there's a fireplace in the basement!"

"Wow! That's fantastic! You're going to be my new neighbors then!"

Carrie looked at the huge three story house behind Jonathan. "*This* is your house?"

He looked sheepish, "Yeah, buying a fixer-upper seemed like such a good idea a few months ago…"

"Are you doing it all yourself?"

"Pretty much. I've had a few guys in to help, but it was more work trying to get the job done right than it was to do it myself."

Carrie smiled. She loved it when perfect connections presented themselves. "I think you might want to pop over and see Chris at the house we were just at. He's done all the work on that house so you can see the quality, and he used to have his own construction company where he did all kinds of renovations. Plus, he's a family guy with a lovely wife and daughter so he's not going anywhere. Here, I'll text you the address. He should be there again tomorrow."

"Yeah!" Katie piped up, "Becky's my friend and Mommy babysits her sometimes but she had an accident because Mommy didn't know she wanted to pee!"

Jonathan raised an eyebrow and looked at Carrie. "Chris' daughter Becky's special needs, and I missed her cue that she needed to use the bathroom," she explained. "My fault, not hers. And Katie, honey, that's something that's over so let's not talk about it anymore, OK?"

Katie's face fell. She had been warned before not to talk about other people.

Jonathan watched the two of them for a second, "I think I'd better go have a chat with Becky's daddy before he gets snapped up for another job. When are you guys moving in?"

"Probably next week sometime, as soon as Chris is done. It's really nice inside!"

"That's perfect! I'm so glad to hear your housing is all sorted out." Jonathan did his best to look excited for them and hide his disappointment. Carrie didn't know that Jonathan had planned to get his own place livable for her and the kids and he was going to move back in with his brother. He just wanted to make it look a little less 'fixer upper' before he suggested it to her. It looked like he was already too late.

"I was going to rent a big truck next week to take a load of stuff to the dump. Let me know when you need it, and I'll get some of the guys and we'll help move you over." He winked at Katie, "I've been waiting for some cute new neighbors!"

Carrie barely registered the offer to help move. She hadn't even thought of having to pack up the whole house for moving! And now she barely had any time, plus she still had Kara's boys this week. She groaned out loud.

"You OK?" Jonathan reached out and put his hand on her shoulder. She closed her eyes for a second before answering.

"I just realized how much work I have to do! We'd better get going!"

"Alright. As soon as you have a moving day set let me know!" Carrie nodded and they said goodbye before heading back to their old house, her mind spinning with everything they needed to do. Katie was upset about missing seeing the new park, but she was partly appeased by knowing they'd be living right by it soon. Once inside she sent the kids to use the bathroom and grab a snack.

Pulling out her phone, she dialed the housing number. When she explained that she could be out of the house by the end of next week the lady on the other end was silent for a moment. "You didn't have to move right away you know." Carrie was glad the lady couldn't see her roll her eyes in full-on annoyance.

"However, we've got a family on the waiting list who are expecting a baby in two weeks. Now I can tell them they'll be enjoying their baby in a home instead of the shelter. Let me know as soon as you know for sure when you're moving out. I'll have to perform the move out inspection. The list of things you need to do is in your lease agreement."

Carrie couldn't imagine the stress of expecting a baby and not having a home at the same time. She made a mental note to do something for the family after she had moved. Then she sent a group text to everyone to say they were moving and give the new address before gathering up the kids to go get some empty boxes from the grocery store.

But by the time they were home again, she just couldn't bring herself to do anything else. Suddenly it seemed like there was just too much to do, and she didn't have the energy to even try to start. She forced herself to make a simple supper of sandwiches which they ate in front of the TV.

She made a hot chocolate for Matthew after Katie was in bed, and they sat at the table to talk.

"Did you get in trouble for watching kids or something Mom?"

"I didn't, but I could have. I didn't know that you weren't allowed to run businesses out of your house if you lived here. It's strange, because the lady I dealt with when we moved in knew that I'd be babysitting the boys because that was my guarantee I'd be able to pay the rent. She didn't say anything. But even if that was OK, selling the frames would definitely be considered running a business, especially with a website set up and everything."

"But won't they get mad at you?" Matthew had spent the first nine years of his life watching his dad get mad at his mom. It was something he was very sensitive about, and Carrie suspected it was the reason he tried so hard to never break a rule.

She took his little hand in hers. "Matthew, listen to me. It's impossible to be perfect. We're all going to make mistakes and have to deal with the consequences. But this wasn't done on purpose. I found a good way to take care of my family, by babysitting and making frames, and I'm really proud of myself for doing that! If I had to go back, I'd do it again, even if it got me in a little bit of trouble!"

"You would?" His huge eyes and gaping mouth were almost funny.

"You bet! And the thing is, because I'm making more money, I can pay to get that new house for us! Which is a pretty good thing, don't you think?"

"It's too bad I can't get a dog yet, but at least now we have a nice house. Do you think I could invite some friends over after school starts?"

"Definitely! We'll make that basement into an awesome hang out zone and you can have friends over lots! But right now I think you'd better get some sleep. It's going to be a busy week for us!"

"OK." He went to put his empty mug in the sink.

"Matthew?"

"Yeah Mom?"

"Leave the mug on the table tonight, just so you can break a tiny little rule before you go to bed."

He smiled at her before turning and putting the mug back on the table. Giving her a big hug, they said their 'I love you's' and he went to bed.

Carrie got out her laptop to check on her finances before she went to bed. It was no small miracle that she had enough to pay for the rent and the damage deposit earlier. Sure, it required taking all of next year's grad school savings and putting them in her checking account *and* using part of her emergency savings, but even after that she still had a small emergency fund of $550 left over. That might be spent getting things hooked up at the new house. But at least for now she was OK. And she was still glad she had done all the back to school shopping. That one day of not worrying about money probably wouldn't be repeated again for a long time!

She went to bed with thoughts of the new house going through her head. It was pretty easy to picture where the small amount of furniture would go, but it was going to be *so* nice to have more room. And a bedroom of her own! Bliss! It gave her renewed inspiration to get going on more frames. She wanted to make this house nice, and if there was any way to make a little extra 'extra' cash then that's exactly what she'd do!

CHAPTER 16

On Saturday Carrie's alarm shook her out of a deep sleep. Quickly turning it off so as not to wake Katie, she only let herself lay in bed for a few seconds before getting up. No time to be lazy— she needed to get going. It didn't even occur to her that the night had been free of bad dreams, but the good night's sleep set her up for a productive day. Later on, when she realized the dreams were decreasing in number, it gave her hope that they would eventually stop.

First thing on the list was starting another set of frames. Now that she'd signed a lease, she had to keep on top of her inventory. She couldn't risk missing out on any possible sales. When they were at the mall she'd caught a glimpse of a magazine cover showing a living room with an accent wall that had a collection of empty picture frames each painted a different shiny, bright color. She loved the look and wanted to get something similar listed on her website right away.

By the time she had sorted through all her frames stacked in the dingy basement and picked out seven that were different enough to stand out from each other, Matthew was up. She set down the frames on the table before going to give him a good morning kiss on his head. When she peeked in on him a little while later he had fallen back asleep on the couch. Maybe he could catch all the extra sleep Carrie would be missing this week!

She checked all the frames for damage and sanded any rough spots before cleaning off the kitchen table and putting an old shower curtain down to protect it. Recently she had found a set of thick, short strips of wood at the hardware store on clearance. They were just high enough that she could set frames on them and then paint the entire frame without it touching the table. She carefully primed each frame using her favorite primer. It was the most expensive, but it went on so smoothly that she only ever needed one coat, no matter what she was covering up.

Katie's arrival downstairs woke up Matthew, and all three of them sat on the couch to eat their breakfast. *Was being able to eat a bowl of cereal while on a couch a life skill?* Carrie wondered. If it was, they were rocking it!

"Okey dokey. We have a ton of stuff to get done before we move to our dream house!"

Katie giggled at the name, "Mommy, can I sleep in your new bedroom with you and the other room can be my playroom when we move?"

Carrie tried to answer gently. Even though she was five and quite independent in some ways, Katie loved sharing a bedroom with her mom and Carrie suspected she didn't like the thought of being alone every night.

"Well, I think it's time for you to have a bedroom all for yourself. But maybe we can get a special stuffed animal to share your room with?" She breathed a sigh of relief when Katie quickly agreed with the idea. It felt like her kids had already lived through enough stress to last a lifetime and she really didn't want to bring anymore on them, even if it was something like sleeping in their own bedroom.

After breakfast she sent them each upstairs with a box to pack any cool weather clothes they didn't need for the week. It was only minutes later that Katie came back down the stairs dragging a box bursting with clothes and toys. Carrie turned her around and followed her back upstairs to re-pack.

When it was late enough in the morning that she wouldn't be waking anyone up, she called her family. Good thing she had waited before asking her parents if she could move back in! Now she could tell them happy news—they didn't need to know how close she had come to total desperation.

"Hi Dad! How's it going?"

"Carrie! Good to hear from you! It's going great. Your mom and I are counting the days until next weekend when we see you again."

"Is mom doing OK?"

"She's fine honey. Bragging about you to everyone who will listen, and she's got everyone talking about your new website."

"Good! Does it work to put her on speakerphone? I wanted to tell you both something."

"Of course, just a minute…"

After a few clunky sounds, Carrie could hear her mom's voice. "Hi Care Bear!"

"Hi Mom! So, we've had a few changes around here… Turns out I can't operate a business while I live in the townhouse complex. So we're moving!"

"What on earth? How are you supposed to get out of subsidized housing if you can't have a way of making more money? That's ridiculous!"

"I know Dad, I agree. It was a bit scary to find that out, but the husband of a friend of mine is fixing up a rental house nearby, and now we're going to move there!"

"Geez Carrie, you sure don't waste any time!"

"Actually, this is all credit to a few good friends who were looking out for me. And it's going to work out really well. It's a cute little bungalow that's got fresh paint and flooring," Carrie looked up to see Katie dragging another overflowing box of clothes and toys down the stairs. "Here, I'll get Katie to tell you about it. Katie, come here and tell Grandma and Grandpa about the new house."

"It's beeeautiful!" Katie jumped in, "And there's a dishwasher and a front yard and a back yard and a basement—a really really nice one! I have to have my own room now and that makes me sad. But Mommy's going to buy me a new teddy bear so I don't get lonely! And Uncle Johnny lives nearby so he can come over all the time now!"

"Okey dokey fast talker. Um, how about you go get Matthew so he can say hi too." Carrie took the phone back from her tell-all daughter and had to smile as she tore full speed up the stairs. "Her kinder-garten teacher is going to have her hands full!"

"So, will the kids stay in the same school?"

"Yep, same school, and I think we're still about the same distance away from school and Jenny and Max. And there's a playground right nearby. That will help. Oh, here's Matthew." She passed the phone to Matthew, and he gave a much different description of the house including things like the bathroom and the carpet in the basement.

"I'd like to come up for the day and help you move," her dad offered after chatting with Matthew for a few minutes. "Do you know what day yet?"

"I think it's Thursday or Friday next week. It's really worked out perfect, because Kara's boys will be at her parents for that week so I only have to focus on my business and moving. Well, and then going to see you."

"Well, if it's Thursday, how about I come up for the day and help you move, and then I can bring the kids back here and give you a day on your own to get settled before you come down for the weekend."

"Seriously? That's a great idea Dad! Thank you! Oh, gosh, wait… I don't know…."

"Carrie," her mom had her serious voice on. "It's not healthy to be with them all the time. You know that. Take a short little break, and enjoy the chance to get settled while we get our grandkids all to ourselves. OK?"

She sighed. As usual, her mom was right. "OK, and thank you. That will be really helpful. Well, I think I need to go up and supervise some packing. I'll call Jessica right now and tell her too. I love you guys."

"We love you too!" they said in unison.

After a chat with her little sister, Carrie was feeling good about everything. Jessica had always been the ambitious one, ready to go after anything she wanted. Right now she wanted to be partner in the personal injury law firm she was working for, and Carrie had no doubt she'd do it. The only thing that wasn't fun was how busy Jessica always was. They had hoped to see her in the summer, but it would be Christmas before she could get any time off. She did try to text Jessica regularly, just to touch base or send a picture of the kids, but often it was a week before she'd even reply. It was nice that she had been able to hear her voice!

Setting her phone down in the kitchen, Carrie made her way upstairs to check on the kids' packing. Matthew had almost done his whole room, carefully leaving out enough clothes for every day before they moved. Katie, on the other hand, had tried to stuff as much as possible into a box, and the room had taken on its usual Katie-tornado aftermath.

Together they separated out clothes and toys, and Katie picked the clothes she wanted to keep out. The rest Carrie refolded and Katie was a little bit more careful putting everything in the box. "See, Katie-girl? When we fold everything and put it in carefully we can fit way more in every box. That way it will be less work when we move, and your clothes will still look nice when we unpack them!"

"Alright. Since you two have done such a fantastic job of packing, why don't you have screens for a bit while I get the last coat of paint on the picture frames."

"Do you need any help Mom?" Matthew asked.

Carrie thought for a minute. With the huge increase in rent she had just committed to, she definitely needed more help. Even though she thought Matthew deserved to just veg out with his Nintendo Switch she replied, "Yeah, bud. I could definitely use some help. Do you want to just pick some frames from the basement to bring up and start prepping?"

"Sure Mom!"

Thank goodness she had Matthew to help her! He was careful and meticulous, and with him sanding and priming the frames she could get a lot more done. It hadn't taken long to show him what to do, and he was thrilled with the money he earned for each frame he got ready for her. She hoped her dad was still out collecting more frames while it was yard sale season. That would really help too.

Once they had finished eating another supper on the couch, the brightly colored frames were almost dry enough to set up for photos, but the lighting just wasn't right in their gloomy house. Carrie figured they didn't need a perfect surface because the frames were so eye catching, but in the house the floor lamps would just leave shadows. She looked out the kitchen window onto the backyard. It would be so nice not to have to look at that scruffy weathered fence anymore. But that gave her an idea...

CHAPTER 17

Two minutes later Katie was laughing at Carrie, who was standing at the table with the blow dryer making sure the frames were dry. There was only about an hour before she'd lose the evening light, and she wanted to try hanging all the frames on the fence to photograph them.

Matthew helped by gathering some small nails and the hammer, and together they went out into the backyard they never used, for a photo shoot! The final result exceeded Carrie's expectations. She had grouped the bright frames a couple different ways and taken a half dozen pictures. Against the rough wood the frames looked even more brilliant—and a lot like she remembered the frames on the magazine cover!

They carefully brought all the frames back in and set them on the floor in the living room to dry for one more night. But Carrie wanted them up on her website right away. She decided to price them at $275 plus shipping. If they didn't sell she'd drop the price, but her rent was going to be a lot more from now on, and she wanted to make sure she could cover it without scrambling every month!

When she logged on she was surprised to see two orders waiting for her. She had totally forgotten about her phone for a few hours and look what had happened! After putting the new set up for sale, she got the shipping booked for the other orders. She'd have to pick up more shipping supplies tomorrow before she could pack them up. But that would be a good time to take Katie out to pick a teddy bear. She wondered if she had enough money in the budget to get some things for the new house…No. That was silly. She had just emptied her grad school savings! *Priorities Carrie!*

"You know Matthew, I have a pretty good feeling about these colored frames. Can you help me bring all the frames we have left upstairs so we can make a plan? I'm going to do them all colored like that, and it will make more sense if I do one color at a time."

Thanks to her dad's help earlier in the summer, and the yard sales she and the kids had been to, Carrie still had eighteen small frames and three large ones waiting for a new life.

She stood back and looked at them once they had them lined up. "How about we aim for three sets of the colored frames? I'm sure we can find a few more big ones if we go to some yard sales tomorrow morning, and then we'll have enough for three sets of seven."

"Does it matter which frames are which colors?" There was Matthew, looking for a rule to follow again.

"I know! Let's let Katie choose which colors to paint which frames. As long as there's a good variety, we really can't go wrong. Katie? We need your help!"

Katie came bouncing into the kitchen, "You do? For real?"

"Yep, I need you to use your artistic eye to decide which frames to paint which colors. Here, let's set out the different cans of paint along the floor, and you put the frames in front of the right color for them. Got it?"

"Got it!" She gave two thumbs up for extra emphasis and got to work. Carrie and Matthew shared a smile above Katie's head as she carefully sorted out the frames. It was nice to have both kids helping out this way.

"TA DA!" She spread her little arms wide and presented them with their new challenge.

"Perfect, thank you! I guess we'd better get to work!"

"You're welcome Mommy. Whenever you need me again, you just call me, OK?"

"You bet Katie-girl!"

Together Matthew and Carrie worked at sanding and priming the frames, being careful to leave them organized with the right color of paint. It would be an early morning tomorrow for Carrie, but well worth it if she could get the rest of the sets done by Monday.

By Katie's bedtime the table and part of the kitchen floor were covered with primed frames drying. "OK bud, that's enough for today. How many did you get done?"

"Um…ten sanded and six sanded and primed."

"Holy cow! You're amazing! Unfortunately I'm going to have to pull you out of school so you can stay home and work every day. We'll be rich in no time!"

"Mom…" he pretended to complain but Carrie could tell he was quite proud of his work. She added a credit of $32 into the notebook where they tracked his earnings.

"Go chill out now. I'm going to put Katie to bed."

Carrie had to admit, a part of her was sad about no longer sharing a bedroom with Katie too. There had been so many times when she felt powerless to protect her kids that having them as close as possible always made her feel a little better. But her mom was right. She needed to start giving them some space from her or they might grow up with all kinds of issues!

Carrie browsed on her phone while Matthew gamed. She could

hardly remember what it was like when she only had her old flip phone. This 'new' smartphone had been a hand me down from Jessica when she got her first work phone from the firm. It was nice to be able to keep up with what her small circle of friends was doing, and send the odd text whenever she felt like it. Plus there was the whole Pinterest rabbit hole that she could fall into for hours on end if she wasn't careful!

When it was Matthew's bedtime Carrie was right behind him. She couldn't have stayed up any later, even if she wanted to! Settling into bed with a smile, she mentally walked through her new house again, dreaming of all the things she could do if she had lots of money.

Even though she was exhausted and happy when she fell asleep, the nightmares found her again. At least they didn't make her cry anymore—maybe she was getting used to them. She'd just make her way to her chair and surf on her phone until her heart slowed down and her eyelids started to droop. A part of her was convinced that this was her life was now, and since there was nothing she could do about it, she just had to tough it out. The other part of her still hoped that one day she'd be back to uninterrupted, peaceful sleep *every* night.

CHAPTER 18

Carrie thought moving would be pretty easy once she had packed up everything in the house. But she hadn't counted on the ridiculous move-out list that was included in her lease, or on trying to get as many frames done as possible so she could actually afford her new house. Finally, on Tuesday evening, she posted the three sets of colored frames and started to pack up all her supplies. It was amazing how much she had amassed for her little business!

The first colorful group of frames sold a few days later so at least she knew she was onto something. But it definitely took up space and time for the type of work she was doing! The new landlord had confirmed they could move in on Thursday if Carrie paid an extra $83 for the two days at the end of the month. It seemed a little silly to charge for it, but she bit her tongue and wrote him another check.

Now she just had Wednesday to get the old house completely cleaned and ready for an inspection. She was hoping she would get her full damage deposit back, but with the dragon lady there were no guarantees! Carla had sent her a text saying that the landlord was paying her to clean the new house once Chris was done, so at least Carrie knew she was moving into a clean place.

Of course, when she had made appointments for haircuts she didn't know she was moving, so right in the middle of the day they all lined up for the mobile hairdresser. Carrie had to admit, the kids looked much better with professional cuts, and she was glad they'd go to school looking nice. Matthew's hair was perfectly cut to be styled to the side the way he liked it, and the hairdresser had managed to tame Katie's curls enough to give her hair a nice bob. Now if they were in a rush Carrie just need to pop some hairclips or a headband on her daughter instead of always trying to pull it back into ponytails or a braid.

With a bit of encouraging from the kids Carrie also sat down for a haircut. Since Matthew's birth ten years ago she had worn a ponytail nearly every day because it was the only thing she could do with her unruly wavy hair. But with a bit of magic from the hairdresser she ended up with soft bangs and a shoulder length layered hair cut that she could leave down once in a while.

"Mommy! You just got really really pretty!"

Carrie laughed, "Thanks Katie! I try!"

She thanked the hairdresser and happily gave her a nice tip. Thanks to this week's sales, she could pass a little bit of extra cash on down the line.

That night after the kids were in bed she took one more look at her finances, just to make sure she was OK. Her regular monthly expenses were jumping from $1,200 per month to at least $1,860 per month—maybe more depending on how much it cost at the new house for gas and electricity.

One of the things Jenny had coached her on was to get one month's rent saved for emergencies and then keep adding a little to that every month. That emergency fund had rescued her with her very real housing emergency, but with it gone she felt her anxieties about money creep up and take hold. She needed to get that cushion back as soon as possible, but at least right now she had already paid for September's rent.

Carrie figured if she started by topping up her emergency fund from her August earnings then she'd still have $530 to go towards September expenses. And even though she'd only be watching Kara's boys after school, Kara paid her every Friday so she wouldn't wait long for more money to come in. For that matter, so did Jenny for the housecleaning that Carrie would be starting up again next week. So she was hopeful she could make ends meet—as long as nothing changed.

But she still needed to earn at least $860 from sales every month on top of babysitting and cleaning to cover expenses, and then there was the 'small' matter of $9,000 to pay for year two of grad school. She'd just have to keep a variety of great products on her website.

And in the meantime she was starting grad school next week—something she had totally forgotten about in the commotion of moving!

She'd have to watch out for her textbooks which would hopefully come tomorrow. She hadn't put in an address change yet, so she might be chasing them around if she missed the delivery.

When she went to bed that night she was so exhausted she was sure her brain couldn't possibly come up with any nightmares, but she was wrong. This time Don came to the old house, but it was empty and Carrie and the kids were hiding in the basement. He left, furious. When Carrie woke up she wasn't quite as terrified as usual. Maybe it was a sign and she wouldn't have any more nightmares after they moved.

CHAPTER 19

Moving day! Carrie was just finishing her early morning cup of coffee when her dad arrived.

"Hey Dad!" she reached out and took a second to enjoy a hug before ushering him into the house. As always, his unique smell of Old Spice and engine oil made her feel like a little girl, safe now that her daddy was here.

"So, big day for you! What do you want me to do?"

"Come on in for a coffee first. I'm pretty much ready, just need to pack up the last few things after the kids are up."

The sound of voices brought Matthew and Katie downstairs. It was special to have Grandpa at their house, since he didn't usually go anywhere that wasn't wheelchair accessible for his wife. Plus, the idea of going for a sleepover at their house was exciting.

Just as Carrie was finishing packing up their things upstairs, there was a knock at the door. Katie ran to answer the door and let in their moving crew. Jonathan, Jenny's husband Max, and Chris were all there. Carrie introduced everyone to her dad, and they got to work carrying furniture out to the moving truck that Jonathan had brought.

Her move-out inspection was scheduled for eleven, so they all left to go to the new house while Carrie stayed back to make sure everything was ready for the inspection. Matthew would be in charge of directing traffic at the new house. There wasn't much furniture to move, and Carrie figured they didn't really need her there since there was enough muscle to lift everything.

Half an hour later she was in the car on her way to the new house. After all her power-tripping and posturing, Ms. Sanders barely walked through the house before promising Carrie she would receive a check for the damage deposit in the mail at her new house within the week. Carrie breathed a sigh of relief when she got in her car. Confrontations were never her thing, and she was glad she didn't have to fight for her damage deposit.

At the new house there was a flurry of activity as the guys finished unloading the moving truck. Carrie found her dad in Katie's room putting her bed together.

"Those young guys didn't leave me much to do, so I assigned myself to furniture assembly. You've got some good friends there."

"Yeah, a bit different than the last move, hey?" She could hardly believe that last year it was just her and her dad bringing the little bit of furniture she thought Don wouldn't argue about as she tried to quickly get out of the house.

"Where are the kids?"

"Oh, I think they're running around downstairs. Jonathan brought some beach balls for them to play with while we unloaded." He paused in the middle of tightening a screw on Katie's pink bed and looked at Carrie, "He seems to care a great deal for the kids. Is he a good guy?"

Carrie looked away, "I think he's a really good guy…but it's not like

I have the best judgment. I'm just trying to focus on the kids and my business."

"You're doing a good job Carrie."

"Thanks Dad. Um, I'm going to go check on the kids and then I'll come back and help you."

"Don't bother, you check on the kids and do what you need to do. I think I can figure out a bed or two on my own."

Carrie had to stand aside as Jonathan and Chris carried up the mattress for Matthew's bed. "I really appreciate this. You guys are the best!"

Jonathan looked like he was about to say something, and then stopped. "Not a problem!" Chris answered.

In the basement the kids were both trying to keep beach balls in the air as they ran around the open space. It was going to be so good to have this extra room!

With the unloading well underway she went into the kitchen to set up the coffee maker and order pizzas for lunch. At the rate they were going she'd be able to make a good dent on unpacking before the end of the day, and buying a few pizzas felt like the least she could do.

By the time the truck was empty she had found all her fridge and freezer stuff and put it away, and gotten out plates and cups for lunch. There was enough room for everyone to fit around the table for lunch, and Carrie couldn't wait to have all her friends over in her new bigger space! Kara and Jenny were coming over after supper, and Carla and Lisa were going to join them if Lisa didn't have to work late.

Max and Chris left soon after eating and amid another round of thank you's from Carrie and the kids. Jonathan stayed and helped Carrie move the rest of the boxes and bags into the right rooms. Katie immediately got to 'work' unpacking her toys, but in such a small bedroom it created an immediate mess!

"I think we're going to need to get you some bins for under your bed Katie-girl." Carrie didn't want Katie to have to keep her things in cardboard boxes anymore. Maybe she could find some shelves for the little closet, too. Katie's previous concerns about being alone in a room seemed to have passed and she was excited for her first chance to sleep there after the weekend at her grandparents.

The kids had their old school backpacks filled with everything they needed for the weekend, and Carrie's dad was keen to get going. He didn't like to leave her mom home alone for too long. For a moment when Carrie and Jonathan were saying goodbye to the kids it felt like they could be any normal couple saying goodbye to their kids for a night away. The thoughts that flew through Carrie's mind in the seconds before she realized it made her blush. She busied herself making sure Katie was buckled and had her toys around her until she felt her cheeks cool off.

As soon as the car was out of sight Jonathan turned to her, "What else can I help you with?"

"Are you kidding? You've been amazing. With getting the truck and all the help, I can't thank you enough! I'm set to unpack now and settle in."

"How about coming over for dinner tonight? That way you don't have to cook in the middle of unpacking."

"Oh, um, well the girls are coming over this evening. And you've done so much." It was ridiculous how badly Carrie wanted to say yes.

"That's perfect! Come on over for supper and then you won't have any dishes to clean up before this evening. What time is everyone coming over?"

"Around seven I think…"

"Alright, I'll have something ready for five thirty. Do you need the address?"

Carrie couldn't resist, "Nope, not unless there's another house with a toilet in the front yard."

"Yeah…toilet's gone, and my only attempt at landscaping along with it! I'll text you the address. Don't work too hard this afternoon!" After a brief, gentle hand on her shoulder, Jonathan said goodbye and left.

Carrie found herself watching him walk away before he turned back and caught her staring. He winked and she didn't turn away fast enough to hide her blush. Again. She quickly went in the house to find something to keep herself busy.

Jonathan found himself whistling as he got into the moving truck. *That* had gone well! Sure, she wasn't moving into his house—yet— but having her live so close would give him lots of opportunities to become a part of her and her kids' lives.

Carrie was quite annoyed to find that unpacking boxes gave her mind free rein to think about Jonathan. Every time she managed to focus on something she'd find her mind wandering back to him. The way he had seemed to get along well with her dad, and the kindness he always showed the kids. Matthew and Katie were happy when he was around. And there was no question she liked having him around too.

But, she *had* made a pact with herself when she left Don that she was done with relationships. The shame and pain that came along with the revelation that she had been totally conned into believing he was a good guy was almost more than she could bear some days. If she could be fooled once, she could definitely be fooled again. And that was something she wanted to avoid at all costs.

Despite all that, she found herself looking forward to five thirty. It was tempting to change and put her hair down before walking over but she refused. She didn't want to give Jonathan any ideas.

Walking up the path to his front door she had time to look around more carefully. The house was one of the biggest on the block with two full stories, and cute gabled windows at the top that suggested a charming top floor. There wasn't any landscaping, but the grass was in much better condition than her brown lawn and had been recently trimmed.

She reached up and tapped the knocker twice on the wooden door. Seconds later Jonathan opened the door. "Hey, come on in. Oh, keep your shoes on. Some parts of the house just have subfloor right now."

Carrie walked past him and let her eyes sweep over the main floor. "Wow! This place is huge!" The open plan was rough, but she could already see what a great family home it would be. A living room with one brown leather couch and a TV on a low stand led into a dining room with a folding table that was already set for dinner for two. In the kitchen, gleaming stainless appliances and granite counters set off the cream colored cabinets. Big windows looked out into a back-yard that had a playset and a swing set.

"Would you like a tour?"

"Sure!"

Jonathan showed her around the big house, talking about his plans, and what he had done already. The middle floor had three big bedrooms with a full bathroom and a second living area. Upstairs a master suite was taking shape with a roughed in bathroom and a huge soaker tub waiting to be installed.

"I'm going to have Chris working with me full time when he's finished his current job. That'll help me make some real progress. Turns out living in a construction zone isn't that fun."

"No kidding. Is this your full-time job then?"

The doorbell rang before he could answer. "Let's head downstairs, I'll tell you while we eat. I hope Chinese takeout is OK."

"Anything's OK if I didn't have to make it!"

"Alright. High standards. Good to know." He smirked before gesturing for her to go ahead of him.

Sitting at the table with just Jonathan, Carrie suddenly felt incredibly uncomfortable. What was she doing here? She should be home, unpacking or painting frames! It only made things worse when he looked and saw her clenched hands resting on her plate.

"Carrie, there's no pressure here, OK? I'd like you to at least eat before you run out of here, but if this is stressing you out, I do have a takeout container handy." When she let herself look in his eyes, he smiled, but it seemed like a sad smile. She didn't know what would make him sad, but she didn't want to run home anymore.

Taking a deep breath she forced herself to unclench her hands.

"Are you OK to stay?"

Smiling, she nodded. "I'm OK to stay. Thanks. Um, so," she struggled to create something normal and neutral, "is this house your job right now?"

Opening up containers, he indicated for her to serve herself. "No, the house was kind of a spontaneous decision. I work in online security, but since moving back I've only kept a few smaller contracts. I *thought* that I'd be able to work for a few hours a day, fix up the house a bit at a time, and have lots of time for Angela, Max, and Jenny."

"But this house just turned into a big job. I thought it deserved to get the best, but I didn't realize how much work the best would be until I started tearing out all the old stuff. Once I started I kept seeing more and more that needed changing. That's why having Chris' help will make such a difference. I'm counting on his professional judgment to rein me in a bit so I don't get carried away!"

Carrie looked around, "Well, if it looks promising now, I can't imagine how it will look when you're done. This house just begs for a big happy family!"

"That's what I thought!"

"Oh my goodness, this is delicious. What is it?"

They spent the rest of the meal talking about favorite foods. Jonathan missed the char kway teow, which was a near-daily lunch in Singapore and had tried some pretty strange foods in his travels.

"So, do you miss traveling? I don't think you've gone anywhere except that one trip back to Singapore just after you moved here."

"I've had enough of traveling alone. I'd love to do more, but sometimes when you don't have anyone to share it with it's not very fun."

At that they lapsed into silence for a few minutes. Carrie didn't know what else to say. When they had finished eating, she reached to take his plate and help clean up, but he held up his hand to stop her. "Nope, I got this. After I walk you home, of course."

His hopeful smile silenced her before she said no. "Jonathan, I, um… it's nice to be around you. But it seems like you're hoping for more, and that's not something I'm willing to offer."

He leaned back and looked at her for a moment before speaking. "I know, and that's OK. I see you, Carrie. I see all the goodness you hold inside of you and give to everyone around you. Like I've told you before, you really are an amazing woman and apparently it's no secret that I think so."

Carrie felt her face warming up as she remembered what Kara had said about the two of them.

"I never planned on being interested in anyone again, and I can see that you don't want a serious relationship right now, but I still want to spend time with you and the kids. Of course, I hope you'll fall head over heels for me. But if you don't, I still want to spend time with you."

Letting out a breath she didn't realize she was holding, Carrie had to resist the temptation to reach out and take Jonathan's hand. It wasn't exactly appropriate after the statement she had made. "Well OK, but if you find someone you really connect with, you need to go for it. I'm just not right for you."

"Yeah…totally disagree with you on that one. So how about we just call this a good talk, and I'll walk you home. Wouldn't want the girls waiting for you!"

"Oh my, I forgot about that! Yeah, I should be going. Thank you so much for dinner. It definitely beat the sandwich I would have made at home!"

Jonathan had to fight to not puff out his chest in pride. She had been so focused on their conversation she forgot her friends were coming over! It might be little, but he'd hang on to every hope he could find that one day Carrie would realize he could bring forever love into her life.

At her house he just rested his hand on her shoulder when he said goodbye and walked away quickly once she unlocked her front door. She was worth waiting for, *that* he was certain of.

Carrie took a minute to take in her new house before she took off her shoes. With the evening light coming in both the front and back windows, the whole place felt warm and inviting—even with her ratty furniture! As she went to put her purse in the coat closet she remembered she hadn't pulled her phone out at all when she was at Jonathan's.

Checking now, she was excited to see another order had come through on her website, and her mom had emailed that her dad and the kids had arrived safely and they were all fine. She sent a smiley face reply and saw a message from Lisa that she and Carla would be there just after seven. What a perfect way to end her first day in the new house!

Jenny had promised to bring wine and snacks, so Carrie got to work getting the newest order ready to ship the next morning. Her supplies and frames had been the first to be unpacked after she set up the kitchen, so it wasn't too hard to pull everything together. By the time Jenny and Kara arrived, it was at the door ready for pick up in the morning.

That night, lying in bed in her quiet house, Carrie smiled. It had been so much fun to chat with her friends, and enjoy the wine, fruit and cheese, and brownies that Jenny had brought. There had been some light-hearted teasing when she let it slip that she had eaten dinner at Jonathan's, but they were all happy for her. Her last thought before she fell asleep was that the dragon lady had done her a huge favor. She was going to love living here!

The next morning she woke up feeling confused and disoriented. Laying in a bed—instead of a mattress on the floor—was a strange sensation, and the room wasn't right. As she became more aware she realized she was in Katie's bed. Slowly the memories of the night resurfaced. The nightmare had returned and she had woken up with her heart pounding painfully. Without being able to check on the kids to reassure herself that they were still OK, she did the next best thing— curling up in Katie's bed until morning.

Feeling groggy, she dragged herself downstairs to make coffee. It was early, but she knew she wouldn't be able to fall back to sleep. At least she could finish unpacking and get the house as organized as possible until the frame order was picked up and she could leave for her parents. Her fantasy of enjoying a night on her own had been shattered by the nightmare and she just wanted to be busy enough to forget that feeling of her kids choosing to reject her and go away with Don.

Three hours later, she was finally heading out, but decided to stop at the old house, just in case her textbooks had arrived. Tentatively knocking, in case everyone was still sleeping, she was almost surprised when a very pregnant woman opened the door. Despite her large belly she was terribly thin, with light blonde hair hanging around her face and circles under her eyes telling a bit of her own sad story. Her faded stretched out t-shirt and loose black sweatpants blended into the dirty brown background of the townhouse.

"Hi," Carrie began, "I'm so sorry to bother you, but I'm the tenant who just moved out of this house, and I wanted to see if any mail had come for me? I kinda had to leave in a rush and I didn't have time to change a delivery address. Oh, I'm Carrie by the way."

The woman gave a half-hearted smile, "Hi, I'm Lauren. Yeah, a thing came for you this morning. Woke me up."

"Oh my gosh, I'm so sorry. You must be exhausted with moving and being so pregnant!"

"It's OK. The dragon—I mean the housing lady said we got this place because you left so fast. I guess I should thank you."

"Were you about to call her the dragon lady?"

"NO! No, I—"

"Because that was *my* nickname for her too! She's seriously scary!"

Lauren's face visibly relaxed. "Oh good. I don't want to piss anyone off. We need this place."

"When are you due?"

"Um, the end of next week. Freakin' me out to think about it."

"Don't worry, once it's over everything gets way better! I have two kids now, and I'd gladly do it all over again just to have them." Carrie had to smile as she thought about her kids.

"Really? Cause all I hear is that this is the beginning of the worst." The worried look had returned to Lauren's face.

"Well, it wasn't like that for me, so hopefully it will be really good for you. Do you have a doctor? One of my best friends is a Physician's Assistant at a clinic not far from here if you need one. She's amazing and will totally put you at ease."

Carrie shared Kara's work info, and her own phone number with Lauren. "If any other mail comes, just give me a call and I'll pick it up. And if you're freaking out or whatever, you can totally call me. This house was my safe place after I left my ex last year, so we left lots of good vibes for you." She hoped she was putting Lauren at ease.

"Thanks, maybe I will. I don't really know anyone here, except my boyfriend, and he works up north sometimes so he's not always around. Anyways, if you want your books they're right here. I don't know why you'd want so much reading though. Geez."

"Well, I'm about to start grad school for counseling psychology…" Carrie's voice faded when she saw the two boxes stacked up. "That *is* a lot of reading…"

The two women stood there staring at the boxes for a minute. Finally Carrie found her voice again, "Well, I'm stuck in it now. I'll have to take them in two trips."

When she came back for the second box she reached out to shake Lauren's hand. "It was super nice to meet you! Hopefully you won't get any more early-morning deliveries on my behalf. And let me know when you have the baby, okay?"

Lauren reached tentatively for Carrie's hand, and promised she'd let her know. Carrie braced herself to pick up the remaining heavy box and put it in her back seat before waving to Lauren and driving away. She wondered what it must feel like to be about to have a baby without a support network. Even though Don had been useless, her dad and Jessica had come and helped out when each of her babies were born, and she always had her mom to call when she felt overwhelmed. She was determined to try and be there for Lauren, if she'd let her.

The weekend passed way too fast for Carrie, especially since it represented her last 'free' weekend for a long time. Between going to yard sales with her dad, cooking for everyone, and trying to make a start on her school reading, there was little time to relax. But it was still good to be home, and it renewed her resolve to get through the next two years and keep saving money so one day her parents could join her and the kids in a house big enough for all of them.

CHAPTER 20

The first week of elementary school was a transitional half day for the kindergarteners, so Carrie agreed to watch Magnus and Angela from lunch on, until they started full-time school the following week. Jenny had suggested they try a few days of Angela staying until she could pick her up at five, but after the first day Carrie sensed that school plus an afternoon with five other kids in the house was too much for the sensitive little girl, so Jonathan resumed his early afternoon pick-ups.

They passed his house on the way to the park with everyone later on, and Angela was happy to wave from the window, but Jonathan admitted to Carrie that she refused to go to the park with him when she knew everyone else was there. Carrie assured him that Angela *was* becoming more confident, and eventually she'd be able to handle being around more kids.

All three kids had the same kindergarten teacher, and Carrie was certain she'd have them gaining skills and confidence in no time. It wasn't the same teacher Matthew had, but she had an excellent reputation at the school.

And after one week of coming home for lunch every day, Katie was ready to eat lunch at school like all the big kids did. Carrie was relieved that she had one less challenge to deal with—even though it was a small one. She was already worried that she was in over her head with her own school work.

She thought grad school would be a breeze. With no exams, all she had to do was read, write essays, and use the online class messaging system to leave comments as she completed various readings. But the sheer volume of work, even the first week, was overwhelming. As soon as she walked the kids to school, she came back home, made another coffee, then read and took notes straight through until it was time to pick them up at lunch. On Tuesday and Thursday mornings she worked at Jenny's and had even less time! In the afternoons she did her best to keep working on frames while watching the kids, and then in the evenings it was back to reading until she couldn't keep her eyes open anymore.

She hadn't heard whether Lauren had had the baby, so on Saturday afternoon she made up a little gift basket of fruit and some chocolate and popped over with the kids to say hello. A man answered the door, and seemed pretty grumpy to see them until Carrie explained who they were. His haggard face lit up when he smiled.

"Oh, yeah. You're the chick who gave Lauren that doctor's number. She went to see her yesterday, and they told her everything's fine. She's sleeping right now though."

"Well, we just wanted to say hi and drop off a little gift." Carrie reached out and gave him the basket. "Let her know I'm thinking about her, will you?"

She had to hold the basket out for a minute before he reluctantly took it from her.

"Sh…" he paused and looked at the kids, "Shoot. You didn't have to do this."

Katie saved the awkward situation in typical fashion, "Mommy said growing babies is really hard work and that she'd give presents to all the mommies with babies in their tummies if she had enough money, but we just have a little bit of money so we can only give a present to one mommy, and—"

"—OK Katie, that's enough." Carrie hesitated to look back at the man, but when she did she was relieved to see he was chuckling. "So, I'm Carrie, and this is Katie and Matthew. We really do hope everything goes well and that soon you'll get to hold your little one. And please tell Lauren she's welcome to call or text anytime."

"Thanks. I'm Dustin. Oh, wait, you got some mail." He bent and shuffled through some papers on the floor before passing a few things to Carrie. There was a kindness about him that she didn't often sense in people.

She thanked him and they said good-bye. Walking away, she hoped they'd be OK. It didn't look like there was any furniture in the living room, although there was a small TV on the floor. Going from homeless, to an unfurnished home, to having a baby had to be hard. Next time she came she'd bring some baby things.

Back at home she made a big pot of soup and a casserole to be suppers for the following week, because she just didn't have time to be making something fresh every night. She also had the kids help with getting things ready for their school lunches so there would be less rushing around in the mornings.

On Sunday they all decided to go to the church where Matthew went to Boys' Club. Carrie didn't know if church was something she wanted to do every week, but it was the fall kickoff for all the kid's programs and Matthew wanted to be there.

It turned out to be a good choice. When both Katie and Matthew surprised her by wanting to go to the Sunday School during the service, a little grandma scooted over and filled the space beside Carrie. She seemed to have some sort of calming aura around her, and Carrie found herself feeling comfortable and peaceful, and like everything would be OK.

They stayed for a BBQ lunch, and were surprised when Katie suddenly hollered Angela's name. Inside the big church Carrie hadn't even seen them. She was secretly relieved that Katie hadn't seen Angela during the service — she probably would have worked even harder to get Angela's attention! Having a chance to visit with Max and Jenny was nice, although Carrie had to resist the urge to ask where Jonathan was.

The rest of the day was spent working on frames with Matthew while Katie watched DVD's and colored. She wanted to 'do something' but Carrie decided it was more important to keep her inventory up. Over the week another two frames had sold through the website so at least there was still income coming in. She made a note to call her landlord and remind him of her business. It seemed like he was genuinely interested in some frames, and if there was a chance to make another sale she wanted to take it.

In the middle of the week she got a short text from Lauren, saying she was back home after having a baby girl. Carrie sent her a congratulations message, and added bringing a little gift over to her next week's 'to do' list. She had already decided to go back to her old routine of waking up early in the mornings to get an hour of studying done before she had to wake up the kids for school. At least with her own bedroom she didn't need to worry about waking Katie with her alarm clock, but even on the nights she didn't have nightmares, she found it much harder to get up early in the mornings. She thought longingly back on the summer days when she didn't have to study.

It was tempting to start a countdown for graduating but she figured it was so far away she'd just get discouraged. Maybe the better approach was just to focus on getting through each week and trying to keep up with everything without looking at the big picture. So instead she tried to just focus on whatever the next task was.

When she finally called her landlord about frames, he put her through to his assistant.

"Hi there, my name is Carrie. Jason mentioned he wants a wall in the office decorated. Can you tell me a bit about the space?"

"Of course, it's a wall in the waiting area that's bare right now. I saw some gold-ish frames on your website. Can you do something like that and fill the wall for under $450?"

Carrie was shocked. How did people have the kind of money where they could just throw out some random request like that? It boggled her mind, but she wasn't going to refuse such an opportunity. "Yes, of course! Could you text me the measurements for the wall? I can have something ready in about ten days if that works for you?"

Shortly after, Carrie received the text, and quickly got to work. With Matthew's help in the evenings and on weekends she could get a high-end look together for the real estate office that would be good for her budget and a good advertisement for her business.

She had forgotten to ask if she could leave a little tag on the corner of one of the frames advertising her website, so she'd have to just bring one with her when she delivered the frames, and hope for the best.

Ten days later, she took a break from studying and went to 'install' the frames. She had arranged them at home the way she liked and taken some pictures so hopefully putting them up wouldn't be too hard, and they'd like the finished product. The night before she had a nightmare about breaking the whole wall when she tried to put the first nail up. It didn't give her much confidence as she walked in the door with a large box in her hand!

The receptionist directed her to the empty wall that she recognized from the picture they had sent, and she got to work. In minutes she was so focused on the finished product that she forgot to be nervous. Seeing her work up was a bit of a treat, especially since she had started mailing frames to strangers around the world and didn't have any contact with them.

"Looking good!"

The voice right behind Carrie startled her so much she almost dropped the frame she was about to hang up. Turning around she saw her landlord standing very close to her. She took some large steps away and turned to face the wall. It *did* look good, and with just two more frames to put up, the effect was impressive.

"Oh, thank you! Hey, do you mind if I leave a small card with my website attached to the corner of one of the frames?"

"Sure, if it means you'll still be able to pay the rent." He laughed as if he had made a joke.

"Great, I'm just about finished here. Who should I give the invoice to?"

"Oh, the receptionist will take care of it. She's got a check ready."

Carrie breathed a sigh of relief to know she'd be paid right away. Without knowing how jobs like this worked, she had been hesitant to plan on the extra income.

"Can I take you out for coffee when you're done here? Or maybe lunch?"

"No," she blurted out, "I… uh, I've got a full schedule and I need to get on to the next job." She tried to hide her shock at his request. It felt very inappropriate, although she couldn't say exactly why.

"Maybe another time." He shrugged and turned to walk away, and Carrie quickly finished hanging the last two frames and added the little card with her website address to the corner of a frame closest to the seating area.

The receptionist gave her a sympathetic smile when she walked over. "Don't worry, he's always trying to find his next girlfriend."

"Thanks, yeah, I wasn't expecting that. Anyways, I have the invoice for you. Jason said you had a check ready?" She handed over an invoice for $430, and a few minutes later she was walking away with her biggest payment yet for a set of frames.

In the evening, Jonathan sent Carrie a text:

Can I take you and the kids to a movie this Sunday?

Carrie smiled as she replied:

What? You didn't want to be caught alone in the theater watching a kids' movie?

Sure, it would be a nice break and the kids will be thrilled to go out.

He arrived on Sunday afternoon to pick them up, and Carrie took a minute to appreciate watching him through the window. He was dressed in dark jeans with tan dress shoes, a light grey sweater, and a brown leather jacket. With his blonde hair looking freshly washed and pushed back, he looked like a guy who belonged in a magazine, not coming to pick up a mom and her kids for a movie! As if he sensed he was being watched, he looked up and saw Carrie. With a wink, he jogged up the rest of the walkway and Carrie had to turn away to hide her blush. Again.

When he parked at the theater, Katie piped up. "This isn't our theater! I think you went to the wrong place Uncle Johnny!"

He looked confused. "This is the only theater near us. Which one do you usually go to?"

"The cheap one in the scary neighborhood." Matthew informed him. "But they're only extra cheap once a month so we don't go very often."

"That's my kids! Nothing but absolutely honesty," Carrie chuckled.

Jonathan didn't seem phased. "Katie, you'll have to tell me if the popcorn here is as good as your other theater, ok?"

"OK! Let's go!"

Together they walked into the theater, and Jonathan proceeded to try and get the kids to order what they wanted. But the kids had never been given full choices at a regular theater before. Finally Carrie stepped in and suggested two kids packs. She offered to share with them, but Jonathan turned her down flat and insisted she get something separately. Soon they were heading into the theater with their hands full. Matthew held back to talk to Carrie.

"Mom!" he whispered loudly, "Did you see? This was thirty-five dollars, not including the tickets!"

Jonathan turned back and smiled at Carrie. Yes, it was really nice to be able to treat the kids, even if it was someone else's money! After the movie Jonathan tried to take them out for dinner, but Carrie asked him to join them at their house instead.

Sitting at Carrie's table with the kids, eating her amazing homemade soup and listening to the kids recap their favorite parts of the movie, Jonathan felt like he had finally found his place.

He had been incredibly self-centered when he was younger, expecting that everything would always work out in his favor. Finding out his fiancée had been killed in a car crash nearly destroyed him, but when it came out that she was with another guy and they had been caught on various surveillance tapes drinking at bars across the city earlier, it felt like his spirit died.

For the next few years he tried to bury his pain in work and humanitarian projects. Singapore was a perfect place to hide from everything, until Jenny's cancer diagnosis invaded his bubble. It shook him to realize he might lose the little bit of family he had left. All he could think of was doing everything he could to help Jenny get better, hanging out with his brother, and spending as much time as possible with Angela.

Meeting Carrie the second day after he arrived had given his nearly dead heart an unexpected jumpstart. This time around he wanted to get it right. He knew Carrie was pure gold, he just hoped he could somehow deserve her.

"Uncle Johnny! What was your favorite part?" Katie interrupted his thoughts.

"Oh, uh, the part where we came back here and had supper together!"

Katie giggled. "That wasn't in the movie!"

He smiled at her before turning to Matthew, "So, have your guitar lessons started up again?"

"Yep! Last week. My teacher said he could tell I've been practicing this summer!"

"Do you want to play something for me after supper?"

"Well, Sunday's my day to clean up supper." Matthew got a tiny glint in his eye, "If you help me I'll be done sooner and then I can play guitar."

Carrie tried to avoid making eye contact with Jonathan. She didn't know where he stood on the whole division of labour in the house thing...

"Yeah, no problem."

So, after they finished eating Matthew and Jonathan cleaned up while Carrie and Katie went upstairs to get ready for the week. Katie could take an hour to pick out her outfit for the day, and it usually involved trying on everything in her closet. So now part of their Sunday evening routine was choosing Katie's outfits for the week.

Afterwards, Matthew gave them a mini concert with the songs he had learned. Carrie was amazed at the new skills he was learning and his musical ability. "Gee bud, that's pretty impressive! I couldn't even figure out the recorder when I was in school."

"Actually Mom, I was wondering if I could start piano lessons too. The music teacher said that piano's the best way to learn the basics of music."

Carrie paused before answering. She could probably manage to pay for piano lessons — it would just require selling one more large frame per month — but she didn't have any way of buying a piano. She gave a noncommittal, "We'll see," and then changed the subject.

Later on, she lay in bed thinking about her finances. She *should* be over the moon about where she was right now. The money she earned every month already paid for all her expenses, Matthew's guitar lessons, school trips, and the odd 'new' piece of clothing from the thrift store. It was more than she could have dreamed of a year ago. But she wanted more. Never mind being able to pay for the second year of grad school. She wanted more *now*. To be able to do things like sign her son up for piano lessons and buy him a piano.

The only option she could see was getting more frames done. The website was doing well, even with the limited inventory she had up, and if she could get more frames done, she could increase her earnings. But then her studying would suffer, and if she didn't do well in school everything she had done so far would be for nothing!

CHAPTER 21

By the end of September Carrie had reluctantly accepted that the next two years were going to be even harder than she thought. Even with getting up early and studying nonstop whenever the kids were at school and she wasn't at Jenny's, it was a struggle to keep up. There was just so much reading and writing! Finishing one assignment just meant she needed to hurry up and start the next one.

The student's private online message system helped. It was set up for students in both years of the masters in counseling program to share about their journey through the courses, and their insights about what they were learning. As she read the notes from other students, she was relieved to find out that many were also overwhelmed with the amount of work involved. And almost everyone was starting to see how what they were learning about mental health applied to their own lives in some way. She was shocked at how many students admitted to struggling with anxiety and depression and were either being treated for it or trying to cope on their own. She felt relieved, but it was only after a few weeks of reading other people's insights that she finally felt ready to share her own short post:

I had no idea so many people were dealing with anxiety — I didn't even realize that was what I was going through too! I thought I was just becoming too much of a worrier. I'm hoping to learn strategies that will help me, and then further down the line will help my clients too. I was wondering if anyone else is losing sleep with recurring nightmares? I don't know if it's related to anxiety or something else.

She took Sunday off to focus on the kids and work on frames, and by Monday she was shocked to see how many replies she had. Many people were just leaving short messages of encouragement, but others wrote long replies talking about their own struggles. Although many of them also dealt with panic attacks in the middle of the night, only one also had nightmares:

My doctor sent me to a counselor about the nightmares because I didn't want to start taking sleeping pills, but I was getting sick from lack of sleep. The counselor said that the nightmares were my brain's way of trying to work through an abusive relationship that happened a while ago. I started writing down the nightmares (which at first was really scary) and then talking about them during counseling sessions. A big part of them was a feeling of helplessness so I've done lots of work on becoming more empowered, and having a plan and a script in case I ever see my ex. It's helped a lot. I also went to a support group for victims of abuse for a while, which was amazing because of all the different people I met who had gone through something similar. There's lots of us who have been screwed over by abusers, but we CAN get better and move on!

Carrie added a very heartful '*Thank you!!*' in reply, and sat back in her chair. She wanted to be over Don so she could move on with her life, but she needed to work through some stuff before she could. It was like all the gentle nudges she had been feeling about dealing with her issues all joined together in a single moment. Even if she still didn't *want* to, she felt like she *had* to do something to start to deal with things right now.

With a resigned sigh she grabbed a notepad and moved over to her favorite chair to write out last night's nightmare. Then, she wrote it again, but changed it so that she called Don every name she could think of until he stormed off and the kids ran back to her. She doubted it would change anything when she was sleeping and another nightmare came, but just rewriting the ending made her feel better. Next time the nightmare came, she'd get up and write it out immediately, and then rewrite it to make something terrible happen to Don.

In the middle of everything, Carrie knew that Lauren was still having her own struggles, and she wanted to help. It was challenging to make time to visit her with so much else going on, but Carrie tried to make contact with her every few weeks. Recently Lauren had received a stroller, and she seemed more comfortable coming over to visit Carrie. The first time she came was on a Saturday, and Carrie took a break from painting frames to sit and have coffee with her.

Both kids were enamored with little Brittany, and Carrie and Lauren enjoyed a visit while they entertained the baby. "Just wait until she starts responding to them," Carrie warned, "They'll never let you leave!"

"It's nice to have people so happy to see her. My family lives on the coast and it's too expensive to visit. Not like we'd have room for them or anything."

"Tell me about it. My little sister lives there, and we're lucky if we see her once a year."

"Is that Aunty Jessica?" Katie joined the conversation, less interested in the baby once she fell asleep.

"Yep, that's your only aunty!" Carrie looked over at Matthew. Even though she was sleeping now, Brittany's tiny hand was wrapped tight around his finger, and he looked in awe of her.

Lauren decided to try and go home and take advantage of Brittany sleeping to get some sleep herself. Carrie still remembered the total exhaustion she felt when the kids were babies. Even though Lauren's partner was far more engaged than Don had ever been, it seemed like he was away a lot, leaving Lauren to cope alone.

CHAPTER 22

Halloween! Carrie couldn't believe how fast time was flying. She was managing to make ends meet with her babysitting, housecleaning, and *Framed* sales, and her emergency savings account was back up to one month's expenses—although the grad school account was still a big zero. But with so much time and energy taken up by studying, she often forgot to worry about money until she took a break.

A year ago, she had just enough money to buy costumes for the kids for the first time. This year she was splurging a little bit, and in addition to costumes she bought candy to hand out once she had taken the kids trick-or-treating. Max was working out of town, so Jenny asked Carrie if they could go together. Angela wanted to go out, but she would probably be too shy to actually knock on anyone's door, so it was a perfect solution. Katie would knock on anyone's door and start up a conversation with them too!

She enjoyed chatting with Jenny while the kids walked just in front of them. Katie and Angela were both princesses (no surprise there), and Matthew was a businessman. Carrie guessed he had picked it just so he could dress up. Fortunately she had found a suit jacket at the thrift store that was only a little too big, and she thought he looked very cute—although she knew better than to tell him that!

Long before the kids were ready to be done, she and Jenny decided to call it a night and they said their good-byes and headed home. Matthew helped with handing out candy until Carrie had Katie tucked in, and then they took turns answering the door until all the candy was done. With a sigh of relief Carrie turned off the outdoor light and closed the curtains. She hadn't expected to get any studying done that night, but she still felt a little guilty about it.

Again that night she had a nightmare. They were slowing down in frequency, but hadn't stopped yet. As soon as she woke up she started writing her version of the dream. She had gone through a few weeks of imagining all sorts of terrible things happening to Don—often being hit by a car—but it didn't leave her feeling better. And there was always the kids there, watching. Slowly she had transitioned to a different ending where she directly challenged Don.

"What you're trying to do is wrong, and I won't let you get away with it. Your temper and treatment of the kids is well-documented and I'm willing to face you in court any time. Now, either you let the kids go and you leave, or I call the police."

Although Carrie still thought that the threat of calling the police wasn't enough to actually stop Don in real life, she always wrote an ending where he left, and the kids ran back to her eagerly. After carefully putting the notebook away where the kids wouldn't accidently come across it, Carrie was able to go to bed and sleep until her alarm went off. She smiled when she got up. Slowly but surely she felt that she was overcoming her past, even if she had to put up with some interrupted sleep to get there.

The next afternoon Lauren popped over for a visit. Carrie felt their friendship was real enough that she could keep working on frames while they visited. Even though she should have been studying, she was down to four frames listed on her website, and she needed to get the numbers back up. She was working on two more sets of colored frames. Thanks to her dad's tireless scouring of yard sales over the summer, at least she had the inventory to work with, and didn't need to take extra time to try and scrounge up more frames from the thrift stores.

After taking a few sips of coffee and getting Brittany settled Lauren came over to where Carrie was painting. "This stuff is really cool! I saw something just like it on a magazine at the grocery store a while ago."

"That's probably the same one I got the idea from! As soon as I get a set listed on the website, they sell right away. Trouble is, they're a bit more work than doing an entire set one color."

Lauren inhaled deeply, "God, I love the smell of paint."

"Do you paint?"

"Used to. I totally rocked art class in high school. Was the only thing I was any good at actually. Then I started doing some murals in my hometown. They're still there!"

"Wow, that's pretty neat. Kind of like a piece of yourself will always be at home." They both smiled. "I think I'd be enjoying this more if I wasn't in school too. Every time I do a frame part of me feels guilty for not studying." Carrie tried not to sound too ungrateful. At least she was earning the money to pay her bills. But it was hard.

"I feel ya. Are you sure you want to stay in school? I mean, you could do pretty good with this as your business." Lauren had a point, and it was something Carrie had struggled with—missing out on earning more money while spending money to be in school.

But she had a bigger reason to stay in school. "The thing is, doing frames is just for me. I mean, I suppose people like having them, and maybe it makes their wall look nice. But I'm not *doing* anything important. Not like if I was counseling. There's this huge need out there for what I'm learning, and I want to be part of the solution...I used to think the counseling would be my ticket to supporting the kids, and maybe one day even buying a house. But things have changed. Now, if I keep making enough money with the frames, then

I can just take a counseling job because I want to help, not because it pays really good. So in a way, doing this might help me help more people."

"No offense Carrie, but that's kind of over-the-top do-gooder. It's OK to just take care of yourself you know. You don't *always* have to help people."

"Actually, I think I do." Carrie finished the bright pink paint on a second frame, and stepped back to admire it. This particular color was Katie's favorite. "When I left my ex and was so focused on surviving, a big part of me felt like something was missing. And then I met this lady who was being treated for cancer, and she hired me to help her with housecleaning twice a week. Even though I was getting paid, I felt like I was finally doing something good for someone else, and making their life better. I don't think I can live without that feeling!"

"Geez. Not me. Gotta take care of number one first." She paused and looked down at Brittany, who was gazing at her mom. "Well, I guess she's number one now. But I'm a close second!"

"So," Lauren continued, "Why do you always say, 'counseling psychology'? Isn't a shrink a shrink?"

"Well, I always think of a shrink as a psychiatrist—they're actual medical doctors with a specialty in psychiatry. And then there's two types of psychologists: clinical psychologists and counseling psychologists. As a counseling psychologist I'll do more counseling—obviously—and working with people on day-to-day issues. A clinical psychologist is kind of more chronic stuff and treating serious mental illnesses."

"Uh, sounds complicated. But whatever floats your boat!"

When the kids came home from school, Carrie had finished another set of colored frames. Lauren left when Brittany started to fuss, reminding Carrie to not work too hard. *Yeah right,* she thought.

By evening Carrie had managed to squeeze in completing a few more frames. Seven in a grouping seemed to be the magic number, so if she could get the other colors done tomorrow, they could be listed as soon as they dried. If only she had someone to help her! Matthew was great at prepping and priming the frames, but he was losing interest in helping Carrie, and she didn't want to push him. Just with the work he had already done his savings account was over $240, but he preferred reading or playing guitar to doing messy things like painting frames.

Stopping to heat up a casserole for supper, she let the kids eat in front of the TV so she could catch up on some school reading at the table. She had gotten really good at managing the kids' screen time over the summer, but they were slipping back into old habits simply because Carrie didn't have enough hours in the day otherwise.

That night she lay in bed, trying to calculate how fast she could get the frames done tomorrow so she could get back to studying. There was Jenny in the morning, but if she got up early enough she could have two done before the kids got up. Then, if she was fast getting back from walking them to school, she might get another one done before needing to go to Jenny's. Her mind wandered to Lauren, and her surprising admission about loving art...

Wait! Carrie's eyes popped open. What if she could hire Lauren to do the frames for her? She could still have the final say in what colors to paint the frames, and which ones to put fabric in and which ones to leave open...Could she sell enough frames to pay Lauren *and* make a decent profit?

There were some problems to figure out. Lauren might not want to (although Carrie knew she was really struggling financially). And she might not be able to do it at her house, in case the dragon lady got wind of it and thought she was running her own business. And she'd have to sell more frames every month to make up for having to pay Lauren. But then she could get caught up on studying and actually have time to spend with the kids!

CHAPTER 23

While Carrie worked on painting frames early the next morning, she tried to think about how it might work to hire Lauren—or even someone else for that matter. The thought of having more time to study, and the realization that she just couldn't keep up with doing all the work for her business herself made her acknowledge that it was time to get some help. She had been so used to doing everything on her own. But the idea of having help suddenly made her feel incredibly relieved.

There was still an extra table and chairs downstairs that she had brought when she moved. In her old house, the basement was so cold and creepy that Carrie hardly ever used it. And she liked to do her painting upstairs at this house because she liked being near the kids when they were home. But now, with a cozy finished basement she could relocate down there to study, freeing up space for someone to work on frames upstairs. She stored most of her supplies in the laundry room where they were accessible whenever she was set up at the kitchen table and she wanted to keep it that way. It could work…

Matthew and Katie sat at the edge of the table to eat breakfast, while Carrie stood at the counter. Drying frames took up the rest of the table and part of the floor in the corner of the dining area. But drying frames meant Carrie was closer to sales, so she didn't mind.

Later, as she walked with Jenny after dropping off the kids she brought up her challenges.

"So, it turns out it's really not possible for me to run the business the way I need to *and* do grad school full-time…"

Jenny slowed down and looked at Carrie. "I have no idea how you've managed so far!"

"Yeah, probably not so well. At this point I'm only a few days behind on my studying, so that's not too bad. But I'm almost out of inventory, and that's really slowing website sales. I'm covering my monthly expenses, and my emergency fund is back up to one month thanks to that big job last month. But I only have a few hundred in my grad school account."

"Have you considered switching to part-time school? I think that's what a lot of adults have to do when they've got other responsibilities."

Carrie stopped, shocked. "No, I've actually never thought of that. But I really don't want to. You know this has been my plan—to do the two years of grad school, then my six month internship, then start my counseling business. I'd feel like a failure if I changed it!"

"But would you be? A failure, I mean? If you're running a business that supports you and the kids, and still working towards your degree? I'm pretty sure that's really far away from the definition of failure!" Jenny smiled to soften her words, but she meant it. If only her friend could acknowledge how far she had come and how good she was doing!

"OK, you're right. In this case my feelings are not based on fact."

"Thank you!"

"But I think I'd like to try something else, first. Before I think about switching to part-time."

They arrived at Jenny's house and paused the conversation until they were both at the table for their routine coffee/tea chat.

"Alright, what else are you thinking of trying?"

"What if I hired someone to paint the frames? I'd still decide what to do, and complete the finishing touches, like the ones that need to have fabric put in them and stuff. And I could still do the website listings and shipping. But it's the prep, the priming, and the painting that's killing me."

Jenny got up and came back to the table with a piece of paper and a pencil. "Give me some numbers. How would this work?"

Carrie laughed, "I just thought of it last night! I don't know…"

"Well, how much do you sell your most popular set for?"

"Right now, that's the rainbow colored empty frames. They've been selling for two hundred and seventy-five dollars. I seriously can't even believe people pay that much for a group of empty frames!"

"OK. How much does it cost you? For the whole set, and any fees when you sell them."

"Let's see…Usually fifteen to twenty dollars for all the frames. Unless my dad got them. Then he gives them to me for free. Um, about five for primer and five to ten for paint. And then a one point five percent credit card fee when they sell." She got out her phone and calculated the fee. "That's around four dollars."

"Don't you have to pay for paint brushes?"

"Nope! This summer I went to a yard sale where this guy was selling off stuff from his painting business. So I got a bunch of really high quality brushes for next to nothing. If I'm careful I shouldn't need to buy brushes for a long time!"

"Sweet!" Jenny was quiet for a minute while she added everything up. "So, your cost for everything is about fifty dollars. That means you're making a profit of two hundred and twenty-five dollars for every set you sell. Not bad!"

"Now," Jenny continued, "How about those big frames you do. What's the numbers for those?"

"Well, they sell for a hundred and fifty each. The frames I can usually find for about twenty. Primer and paint is about ten, and whatever fabric I recycled for the inside is maybe ten dollars. Or less."

"OK...Total cost is about forty dollars. So you're making just under a hundred and ten dollars on each one. Now, how much were you thinking of paying someone?"

Carrie looked at the numbers Jenny had written down. "Maybe seventy-five for a set of seven, and forty for the big frames? Then I'm making about one fifty on the set, and seventy on the others. I need to make an extra two hundred and fifty a week on frames to make ends meet. Any extra goes towards grad school."

"I like the idea of paying per piece. That gives you a clear number for your costs. But I think it's a little high. Even changing the numbers a little bit can help your bottom line." Jenny crossed out the numbers and changed them.

"OK, so sixty-five and thirty. Yeah, that gets me to a profit of two hundred forty dollars. *If* they both sell of course. And it's not like Matthew, who has to wait until I get paid for the frames before he gets paid for his work!"

"No, that's true. You'll be out the money for labour before you receive money for the sales."

Carrie glanced at the wall clock, "Jenny? Don't you have your first client in a couple of minutes?"

"Oh, shoot. You're right! Thank you!" She jumped up and headed for her office door before turning around. "You're the best Carrie, always remember that!"

Carrie smiled and turned back to the page of numbers. Was this the solution she needed? Should she just suck it up and keep doing it all herself? Or switch to part-time school? As she got to work cleaning she kept mulling those questions over in her head. By the time she was ready to leave she was no closer to a decision, but at least she had some options to think about. Grabbing the paper and tucking it in her jacket pocket, she popped her head into Jenny's office and waved good-bye before quickly walking home.

No matter what, she had to get those frames done and listed as soon as possible. Hopefully the right solution would come to her soon.

CHAPTER 24

On Friday night Matthew helped Carrie prep and prime two of the bigger frames so that she could finish and list them before the end of the weekend. She thought that it would bump her website listings up enough to feel better about her business. But Saturday morning one of the rainbow sets sold, and her inventory dropped again!

She smiled wryly to herself. It was a bit silly to feel discouraged about getting a sale! She decided that the next step had to be talking to Lauren to see if she was even interested in doing some work for her. In the meantime, she juggled studying with keeping the kids busy for the weekend, trying to clean the house, and making meals for the coming week. Some days there just wasn't enough coffee for everything she needed to do.

At least on Sunday Jonathan invited them over for supper so she didn't have to cook. Matthew and Katie had been over a few times since they moved in. Jonathan had a guitar too, and the two guys liked to 'jam' together. Carrie thought it was terribly cute, and she could see how good it was for Matthew to have special time with a man who didn't yell at him like his dad had. Don had never appreciated that Matthew wasn't a rough-and-tumble kind of boy.

Their back gate was an easy shortcut to Jonathan's and in less than a minute they were at his house. With Chris' help he was making good progress on his remodel. The top floor master suite was breathtaking, and Carrie could just imagine some lucky couple relaxing up there in the cozy sitting area with the fireplace blazing or having a bath together in the double jacuzzi tub while watching the stars through the big skylights on the roof.

On the main floor Jonathan was still waiting to put the flooring in, so he produced a big bucket of chalk and told the kids to go crazy coloring the floor while he finished making supper. Carrie leaned her back against the counter the kids were coloring behind and enjoyed watching someone else cook. She had just finished telling Jonathan her idea about hiring someone to do frames.

"Why don't you get student loans? Then you could just focus on studying." Jonathan knew that someone on her income level would easily qualify for a student loan. And he hated seeing her work so hard to try and make ends meet.

"Not a chance. I'm only interested in getting out of debt, not into it. I know, I know," she stopped him before he could talk, "Your education is an investment and all that. But I hate debt so much. When I left my ex, I ended up with this huge credit card debt that was supposed to be joint, but he never made a payment on it. There were weeks when I had to cut back on what I ate so I could make the minimum payment. That debt impacted my ability to take care of my kids and I swore I'd never get in debt again."

"I hate him!" the low, angry voice behind her startled Carrie, and she turned around to see Matthew standing behind her on the other side of the counter. He had obviously heard everything she had just said —something she immediately regretted. When had he walked over?

Leaning her arms on the counter she place her hand on Matthew's hands that were tightly gripping the edge of the counter. "Hang on bud. Remember what we talked about?"

He shook his head 'no'. Carrie knew he remembered, but didn't want to acknowledge it. "Who's in charge of the choices Don makes?" She couldn't bring herself to call him 'Dad' this time.

Reluctantly Matthew answered, "He is."

"Right. And who's in charge of how you react to things?"

Looking down, and in a quieter voice, "I am."

"And what does hating someone do?"

"It hurts your spirit."

"Matthew, bud, look at me." Slowly Matthew lifted his head and looked at Carrie. "What Don chose to do hurt me, and hurt you and Katie too. But at least we can use that information to help us make better choices. That's why we're careful with money. Because we know how being in debt can impact our family. And that's how we turn something bad into something good. Alright?"

Matthew nodded.

"Come here, you!"

He walked around the counter and let his mom pull him into a hug. She held on until she felt his shoulders relax, and then kissed him on the forehead before letting him go. "Remember, you're the first best thing to ever happen to me!"

"And I'm the second bestest thing, right Mommy?"

"Geez, did you kids grow bigger ears today? Yes, Katie! You're my other bestest thing!"

But Katie wasn't done, "And what about Uncle Johnny? Is he a bestest too?"

"Of course Katie. All my friends are the bestest. But my kids are the most bestest!" She avoided looking at Jonathan. He'd probably take that statement and run with it if she let him.

Clearing his throat, Jonathan took a second to give himself a shake.

He felt like he had just witnessed an intimate family moment that he didn't have access to. Trust Katie to try and include him anyway.

"So…who's ready to eat?" They moved to the dining area where the folding table was set for four people. It was a bit crowded with them all there, but in a nice way. The barbequed chicken, corn, and green salad was delicious, and Carrie teased him about his secret cooking skills.

"You know, we could easily pop over for all our meals. It's not like you're far away!"

Looking her in the eye he smiled, "I'd like that!"

"YAY!" Katie shouted, "Supper at Uncle Johnny's every day!"

"No, no, wait!" Carrie laughed. "I was *joking*! But this is really good!"

"Who wants ice cream for dessert?"

They helped clear the table and then came back for ice cream bars. Then Jonathan suggested the kids watch TV while he and Carrie had coffee. The novelty of cable TV had their full attention while Carrie and Jonathan talked quietly.

"I didn't realize you had to deal with past debts, too. I'm so sorry."

"Yeah, and I've got student loans from a while back too. That's on me. But since I didn't graduate I wasn't able to take advantage of the higher earning potential that can come from a degree." She didn't even like talking about those student loans and the choices she had made.

"Why didn't you graduate?"

"I married Don after third year, and it just seemed like too much work to be married, work, and try to do school. And he really convinced me it wasn't worth it."

"Wow."

"Yeah, I know. But like I told Matthew, it's something to learn from and never do again!"

"All that stuff you were talking to him about. You know, what you can control, and making your own choices. That was some seriously epic parenting there. Where did you learn it? Was that how you were raised?"

"Not really. I mean, it was a pretty powerful lesson to see how things can happen outside your control after my mom's accident. And my parents really drilled it into us that we had to focus on what we had, not what we wished we had…But it was from these two books I read in second year about this thing called Choice Theory. Really good stuff about how we can only control ourselves, but we have all the power over ourselves. It's weird, I applied it to everything in my life —except my marriage. Somehow I really thought it was my job to always cover for him, and try to help him instead of leaving him to fix his own life."

"That's what still messes with me," she continued quietly. "When it came to a relationship it was like everything I knew to be right and good I threw out the window to try and please Don. I missed so many signals that things were really bad, and then it was almost too late to get out. I just don't trust myself in that area anymore."

Jonathan took a slow drink of his coffee before answering, "But it sounds like he had a really manipulative personality. So maybe it was more about him being devious than you being wrong? Plus, sometimes it's easier to believe what you want to about the person you've decided to spend your life with than to face facts."

Carrie thought maybe he was also thinking about being betrayed by his fiancée. "So, we've both proved that we can be fooled…"

"Yeah, but that doesn't mean we have to miss out on something real when it comes along." He smiled at her.

"Maybe…maybe."

They sat beside each other, both wrapped up in their own thoughts.

She wanted to be sure that it was OK to consider a new relationship but didn't have any idea how to go about being sure. Meanwhile Jonathan tried to keep his focus on how nice it was to sit close to her while his mind wished they could do more than just sit beside each other.

It was Matthew who broke the spell when the funniest videos show they were watching ended. "Mom? How long did you want to stay?"

"Oh, um, I guess we should head home. We still need to get lunches and outfits ready for the week." They gathered up their few things and said their goodbyes. Carrie admitted the meal far exceed her expectations.

"Now you know that I'm a great cook *and* I can rock a takeout order. Total package, right?"

"Yeah, yeah" Carrie laughed. While deep inside she agreed. He did seem like the total package.

CHAPTER 25

Carrie was more than thrilled the next morning when Lauren texted to see if it was a good time to visit. When they arrived, Lauren handed Brittany over to Carrie so she could get her own shoes and coat off, and they all went into the kitchen.

"You'll have to get your own coffee. My hands are full!" Carrie joked as she sat to unwrap Brittany from her blanket. She wondered if Lauren even had a winter coat for her. Too bad all of Katie's little clothes were long gone. It would have been nice to have someone to pass them on to!

Lauren brought over coffees for both of them and smiled at Brittany. "She slept through the night last night. I feel like I have superpowers this morning!"

"Yay!!" Carrie was delighted to get a response from Brittany. Baby smiles were the best! "So, while you're feeling so amazing, I have a question for you…" Carrie was distracted by Brittany spitting up. "Whoops!" She got up and grabbed a clean wash cloth.

"Sorry about that. Do you want me to take her?"

"Not a chance! A little baby spit up doesn't scare me." She gently cleaned Brittany's face, and then tucked another washcloth under her little chin, in case there was more to come.

"What did you want to ask me?"

"Oh, right. OK. I know you've got a newborn, and you're on your own a lot. But, I'm realizing that I can't keep up with my business on my own anymore. Is there any chance you'd be interested in working for me a bit every week, painting frames?"

"What do you mean?"

Lauren seemed instantly suspicious and Carrie couldn't understand why. "I need to hire someone to prep, prime, and paint frames for me. I know it's not the same as doing beautiful art or murals, but it does involve brushes and paint. You could fit it around Lauren's schedule. Pretty much everything I finish and put on my website sells, so even if you did a few frames a week it would really help me keep up with demand."

"How do you know I could do it good enough?"

"Well, you do have some art training, which is more than me. And I can show you exactly what works for me so you're starting off on the right foot. I've even had Matthew do some of the prepping and priming, but doing the final coat does take a bit more skill. I really need to do more studying, so I'd probably be in the basement working at the table there when you're painting...if you want to. No pressure. You've got a lot to handle just with Brittany and your house."

"Could I, like, try one sometime for free to see if I'm any good? I don't want to screw up your business."

"I guess so. But I think you'll be fine, honest." Carrie figured she'd just pay Lauren after it was done. Hopefully after she did one she'd feel more confident.

Slowly a smile grew, "Yeah. I'd like that. Ever since last week I've been dreaming about paint and paintbrushes!"

"Fantastic! Do you want to just go with the flow at first, and you can text whenever it's a good time to pop over? Oh, that's another thing. I'd be happy for you to work on stuff at your house, but the lease is pretty clear about not running a business from your home. That's actually why I had to move so fast, because I had the babysitting and the frame business and I was afraid the dragon lady would evict me if she found out."

"Oh, no. I'd much rather do it here and leave everything here. Maybe if I came during Brittany's nap time I could put her on the couch while I painted?"

"Of course, or on my bed upstairs. I just sleep on a mattress on the floor so there's no chance of her falling off the bed."

"You don't sleep on a bed either?" Lauren looked shocked.

"Not yet. Maybe one day when I can afford one. The kids have good beds, so that's really all that matters. Oh, the only thing is timing — you have to let the primer dry before you paint. So each frame will take more than one go to finish. But as soon as it's finished I'll pay you for each one."

"Cool. Uh, thanks for thinking of me."

"You're welcome. I'm excited about it! Now, I'm going to set my timer for fifteen minutes so we can relax and chat and then I have to get back to studying."

She enjoyed learning more about Lauren. Although she came across as rough around the edges, Carrie suspected she had lived a hard life, and was just cautious about everything. Hopefully painting frames would be fun for her!

Before she left, Lauren asked if she could come over the next day in the afternoon to start a frame. Carrie was happy to agree. And tomorrow morning she could tell Jenny that she was one step closer to taking some pressure off herself, *and* helping someone else out.

The next day Carrie had the work space set up for Lauren ahead of time.

Her trusty old shower curtain was protecting the table from paint drips, and the big frame she chose to start with was sitting on the little blocks of wood that lifted it just a tiny bit off the table. She had also gotten out the soft white paint that would finish off the frame after it was primed, and the old quilt she had found that she would cut down to put in the frame, so Lauren could see how the whole project would come together.

Normally quilts were too expensive to use in her frames, but this one had a huge stain on one side and had been a bargain at $10. Carrie loved the different floral fabrics that had been used in the quilt, and the texture would show well inside the frame that didn't have any glass in it. She couldn't help running her finger over the finishing stitches on the quilt. It was just beautiful.

After a quick introduction Carrie went downstairs to study, leaving Lauren on her own. She didn't want to make her nervous by hovering.

Shortly after, Lauren called down, "Hey Carrie?"

"Yeah?"

"Could I put a CD in your player? Would the music bother you?"

"For sure! No bother at all!"

Expecting to hear some sort of heavy metal music, Carrie was surprised when the sounds of a violin concerto drifted down the stairs. It was nice, and a perfect track to study to. Half an hour later, Lauren came down to tell her the frame was primed. As expected, she had done a perfect job.

"I haven't washed the brush yet. And Brittany's still sleeping. Do you have some other frames that need priming? It's kinda dumb to just do one."

"Oh, yeah. For sure. The only thing is that I don't have another surface to put frames on, since that one takes up so much of the table."

"I can work from the floor if you have some newspapers to lay down."

Carrie paused her studying to get Lauren set up again. They agreed to do two medium sized frames that Carrie wanted to leave empty. The bright green, glossy paint she would finish them with was one of Carrie's favorites, and would make the details on the frames really pop.

Lauren didn't quite understand what Carrie was wanting until Carrie showed her a picture of another pair that she had already sold. The brightly colored empty frames really made a statement. "This is so cool!" she enthused.

Going back downstairs Carrie made a mental note to have more stuff ready for Lauren next time. She'd have to be more organized so she knew ahead of time what to ask for.

At the end of the day she felt good. There were frames that would be ready to list as soon as Lauren put the finishing paint on. She had gotten way more studying done than if she was the one doing the frames, and Lauren left looking happier than Carrie had ever seen her. Matthew had come home extra happy from Boys' Club because the director had found out he played guitar, and offered him a chance to play during their family Christmas party the next month. And the thought of Christmas coming up made Katie even more enthusiastic about life.

With the help of the online school message board, and some of the classes Carrie was taking she was learning that her anxiety and worries were actually pretty common, especially considering all the stress she had been under during her marriage to Don. It was abuse, plain, simple, and ugly.

All the ways he had undermined her, put her down, and blamed her for anything that went wrong *were* abuse, even though she and the kids never had bruises or broken bones. It felt OK to accept that they had all been living in an abusive situation. What was harder to accept was how that impacted her and the kids now. She was still wounded inside, and she needed to work on facing those wounds once and for all, and then leaving them in the past. Only then would she truly be able to focus on growing and changing into the person she wanted to be.

She took the big step of talking to Matthew's teacher after realizing that he was probably feeling the effects of the past as well. Carrie expected it to be hard to convince the teacher that her best student might need some help dealing with his past. Instead, the teacher was amazing and understanding.

"While I always appreciate Matthew's willingness to help and his eagerness to please me, I have noticed that he tends to hold back when the rest of the class gets carried away. I'm sure in some cases that would be ideal, but maybe for Matthew he needs to know it's OK to make mistakes."

"That's what I've been trying to work on with him," Carrie admitted. She felt her eyes start to sting over the teacher's kindness and sensitivity.

"There's a program we offer at the school where the counsellor spends time with small groups of kids once a week and they work on developing resilience after difficult situations. Some of them are struggling with things like chronically ill siblings, the death of a family member... things like that. I think it would be good for Matthew. Would you like me to refer him to the program?"

"Yes please. And thank you!"

"Fortunately they're providing more training for teachers about our student's mental health. A few years ago I wouldn't have understood what you were talking about!"

Carrie greeted the beginning of December with a smile. The run-up to the holidays was much easier on her with both kids in school full time. Sure, she still had to deal with hyper kids in the afternoons, but the two-and-a-half hours were manageable. Now that she had more time to study, along with the income that Lauren helped bring in, she was finding that everything was feeling a bit easier and looking a bit brighter.

Lauren was working out better than Carrie could have imagined. Her eye for color was perfect, and she was starting to choose her own combination of frames, colors, and fabrics, leaving Carrie even more time to study.

On average Carrie was paying Lauren $200 per week, and her sales were up to almost $650 per week. It was as she'd hoped—the higher the number of interesting pieces she had listed on her website, the more sales came in. And one of Jenny's clients had insisted on buying the frames that were on the wall in her office, so Carrie put one of her rainbow sets up in its place—which sold a few days later!

Her grad school account had finally passed the $500 mark. Not perfect, but at least it was growing. And for the second year, Carrie's business was making enough money that she could buy Christmas presents for her family. That alone made it all worth it!

Somehow, in the past few months, spending Sunday evenings with Jonathan had become a thing, and it gave Carrie a much-needed break before starting another busy week. The last Sunday they had gone skating and then out to McDonald's for supper. Carrie insisted on paying, "This one's in my budget!" and they had sat and talked for almost an hour while the kids played in the play place. She knew that Matthew would probably outgrow such things soon, but at least for now he still liked it.

CHAPTER 26

Sunday evenings were also the highlight of Jonathan's week. When he was with Carrie and the kids he felt like he fit in a family. After losing his parents and then Cindy, he hadn't expected to experience anything like this.

And while he was completely laid back on Sundays, the rest of his week had changed dramatically. Hearing Carrie talk with such conviction about getting and staying out of debt forced him to take a good look at his own finances.

He'd always earned good money, but he never thought about how he spent it, or whether he needed to change anything. If there was money in his account, he was happy. And since he had automatic withdrawals to cover his bills, he didn't really think about his bottom line.

But he realized that his level of debt would cause worries for someone like Carrie. So he decided to make some big changes. First he started following some money management bloggers. Most of them were his age or younger, and they were all focused on achieving financial independence and retiring early—something he had never considered.

Next, he partnered with Chris to flip a house that was just a few streets away. It was pretty rough looking, but Chris assured him that the structure was solid, and all the problems were cosmetic. After covering the down payment, he didn't have money to pay Chris to work on either the flip or his own house, so both of them were doing what they could around their other day jobs.

His own house was supposed to be an investment too, but now that Matthew and Katie were starting to feel at home there, he was having second thoughts about selling it. So while it sat waiting for more work, he focused his attention on the other house. He was hoping for a big payout from a flip so that he could confidently plan for the future. And if he had anything to say about it, that future would include Carrie, Matthew, and Katie.

For the first time in years, Jonathan was doing manual labor. After Chris finished all the drywalling, Jonathan took over priming and painting. Although all that only happened after he spent three days hauling junk out of the house. He *had* come across some decent furniture that he thought Carrie could use, but he didn't want to tell her about the new house until it was ready for selling, just in case things didn't work out right away. So he just put everything in his garage. If she wondered why he was parking his car out front all of a sudden, she didn't ask.

He and Chris were on target to list the house just before Christmas. Sure, it was crappy timing, but they hoped that someone would want a move-in ready house. If not, they could carry the mortgage costs for a few months until it sold, and then they'd split the profits. That would allow him the chance to either re-invest the money in another flip, or pay off his debts. And it would give Chris the beginning of the money he and Carla needed to start another business.

Jonathan had also agreed to some new work contracts. It had been nice to slack off when he moved back, and take a break from the demanding schedule he had created for himself after Cindy's death. But now he had a good reason to work hard. This time he was running towards something, not away from it. In the first month he made a big extra payment on his student loans. Before Carrie, he had hardly given them a thought. Now, he was determined to get them out of the way as soon as possible.

The advantage to doing manual labor every day was that he was sleeping better. Nights had been his nemesis for years—the times when regrets and insecurities haunted him until the sun came up. Now the only thing that might keep him awake were the aches and pains from working so hard. And it didn't take long for sleep to take over, even then.

He was also enjoying getting to know Matthew and Katie better. If Jenny needed him to watch Angela and he had his own work to do, he'd just invite Katie over too and she'd keep Angela more than busy. While he loved Angela dearly, he found that sometimes her quietness left him worrying that she was upset. With Katie he always knew where he stood—that girl wore her heart on her sleeve at all times!

Matthew was almost the opposite of Katie, but in many ways he balanced her out. Jonathan didn't think Matthew ever said anything he didn't mean. Every word was measured and thoughtful. He actually reminded Jonathan a bit of his own dad, which was bittersweet. If his parents were still alive, they would have been over the moon about Matthew and Katie. At least they had met Angela before they died. And at least they died together. They had been true soulmates and Jonathan's only respite from his grief when they died was knowing they'd never be apart.

He had finally confided in Max and Jenny his feelings for Carrie. Apparently it wasn't a secret at all, and everyone was confused about why they weren't officially dating yet. "It's complicated," he admitted. "We both feel like we've used really poor judgment in the past, and neither of us wants a repeat."

"Seriously Jonathan," Jenny rolled her eyes, "Carrie's a thousand ways better than Cindy. And I know you'd be perfect for her. But I guess she's still dealing with the after effects of an abusive marriage."

"Abusive?" Max felt his pulse starting to race—it was the first time

Jenny had talked about this with him. "How could anyone hurt her? She's one of the nicest people we know."

"Oh, he was too smart to hit her. He just manipulated her, blamed her for all their troubles, and constantly put her and the kids down. I think the more she does in her course the more she realizes how bad it really was. She's said a lot of times that if it wasn't for the loving parents she had growing up, and knowing what a good marriage looked like, she might never have left. The sad thing is that I think a lot of women just don't think there's a better life for them so they never leave."

Jonathan's heart hurt for what she had gone through. "I knew he was an asshole, but I didn't know it was that bad. Thanks for telling me. I want to give her time to be ready for a new relationship and not make her feel pressured."

Max laughed. "My over achieving big brother being patient and self-less? I believe pigs can start flying any time now."

"Ha ha. I've always had a heart. I just didn't know how to use it until I met Carrie."

"Aw!" Jenny bumped her shoulder against his. "I think you're in love! And I couldn't have picked a better woman if I had tried. Did you know it took her two years to save enough money to be able to leave him? I can't even imagine what she went through."

"No wonder she's so careful about money. Although having that new girl helping her out with the painting has really taken some pressure off her."

"Yeah, Carrie's got some good business smarts. She's already thinking of expanding the business into some sort of charity after she graduates so she can give more women a chance to escape poverty. I don't need to tell *you* what an amazing woman she is though."

Jonathan smiled, "No, you don't. But I like to hear it anyways."

CHAPTER 27

"Hey you two, come on in!" Carrie opened the door wide for Lauren and the stroller carrying Brittany to come in. They brought a blast of icy cold weather with them.

"Holy, that was a freezing walk! I swear Carrie, if you lived any further away I'd quit!" She rubbed her hands together to warm them up while Carrie lifted Brittany out of the stroller.

"Oh my goodness, that is the cutest snow suit I've ever seen!"

Lauren smiled proudly, "I've been putting a bit of everything you paid me aside until I could finally buy her some new stuff. The outfit underneath is new too, and I got these great bibs that look like bandanas. They're so cute!"

"Are you still chucking your food Brittany?" She was already getting a reputation for spitting up on anyone who held her. Carrie turned to Lauren, "Did you see Kara about it?"

"Yeah, she said there's no huge problem because she's gaining weight. But I think it's me. It's not like I eat super healthy. Kara did give me some free samples of a formula that's supposed to be good for babies with sensitive tummies, but I want to feed her myself as long as possible."

"Good for you! But once she's OK with a bottle, maybe you and Dustin could leave Brittany with us and go out on a proper adult date!"

Lauren looked up from the boots she was still trying to untie, "Seriously?"

"Of course! The kids adore her, and it's not like she's a difficult baby."

Lauren snorted, "Tell me that in the middle of the night! But hey, I might take you up on the babysitting thing. Dustin was just home for a few nights before he went up north again. It sucks."

Carrie wondered how Dustin could work so much and yet they still struggled with money. But she was trying not to be judgmental. Lord knows, she wasn't exactly the money mogul.

"He's got a problem you know." It was as if Lauren could read her thoughts.

"I'm sorry. I didn't know. What do you mean?"

"I wasn't going to tell you. Ever. Because we're friends…"

"Lauren, it's OK to tell friends stuff. Even if it's bad stuff."

"It's drugs!" She blurted out. "He's a fuckin' drug addict!"

"Oh Lauren," Carrie put her free arm around her friend, shocked and devastated. "I'm so sorry. That must be so hard on you."

Finally getting her boots off, Lauren turned away from Carrie and leaned against the wall. "Especially since it's my fault."

"Here, come sit on the couch." They sat down, and Carrie offered Brittany back to Lauren. She suddenly looked so dejected. "What do you mean?"

"Dustin wasn't really a partier before me. I was crazy. I'd try anything, and it never bothered me after. When I met him I thought I was helping Dustin by hooking him up with some good stuff. Only he couldn't stop once he started. Not like me. I deserve to be the one suffering withdrawal every time he tries to quit. It kills me what he goes through. He's not a bad person Carrie, I promise!"

"I believe you. And I don't think any differently of you, even knowing this. We all screw up Lauren. And you had no idea things would turn out like this. I know how much you love him and how much he loves you and Brittany." Carrie found herself starting to cry, "That's more than me and my kids ever got from Don. You may not believe it, but you're so lucky that way."

"Oh, fuck babe. I didn't mean to make you cry!"

Carrie laughed through her tears, "Watch it, her first word might be a spicy one!"

"Shit. I mean…Yeah. I gotta clean up my mouth. How come you don't swear?"

"Probably because my parents never did. It just wasn't in my head. And with someone like Katie around who remembers *everything* I say I have to be careful anyways."

"I'm trying to do it less. Uh… it's OK you know... And you see Dustin isn't a bad guy. That's actually the reason my family never visits. Because they don't get addiction. They think if he just tried harder he could fix himself. Assholes. I mean…um…jerks."

"Doesn't quite come out the same does it?"

"Not even close. OK, I'm done talking about shit. Sorry. How are sales?"

Carrie started talking over the recent frame sales with Lauren. Together they were figuring out which frames sold best, and which ones to change the prices on.

"Not bad. Another colorful set went on the weekend, and before that we sold those three shabby chic frames that you hated so much. But the big news is that a lady who used to buy a bunch of stuff from me just called with a big order! She wants a set of fifteen empty frames done with the antique gold look."

"Wow! How much wall space does she want to cover? And do we have enough frames?"

"It's a nine foot by five foot space. I managed to get a box of frames off the Buy and Sell site for ten bucks, so I hope we'll be ok. Can I leave you to play around with them and choose the best ones? I have a couple more papers to finish writing before I can take Christmas off."

"Geez Carrie. I don't know how writing papers will make you a good counsellor. Maybe you should just quit school and start your own practice now? You're way better than any of the idiots that have tried to help Dustin."

"Hey! Easy on my future colleagues," Carrie joked. "And thanks for the vote of confidence. I really hope that I learn enough to help Dustin. Maybe when the timing's right you can tell him I know and I still think he's a great guy, hey?"

"I will Carrie. Thanks."

"Hey, earth to Carrie. I'm going to head out now. The frames are all primed, so I should be able to finish them in a couple of days."

"Oh, wow! What time is it? Shoot! I gotta get snack ready for all the kids! Thanks so much Lauren. I could *not* do this without your help!"

"Anytime babe! See ya later!"

Carrie finished the last paragraph she was writing, saved the document, and closed her laptop. After editing this paper she only had two more to write and then she'd be finished her first semester! She was so close to getting a break she could almost taste it!

True to her word, Lauren had the frames done three days later. They were more labour intensive than the usual frames because they had a layer of gold paint followed by a layer of black. Then some of the black paint needed to be sanded off for the gold to show through. Lauren worked hard to get them done, and they both agreed that the finished product was fantastic.

Carrie was delighted to see Eleanor. It had been months since she had sold anything to her first and favorite customer. Even though she had raised her prices, Eleanor was more than pleased with the finished product, and Carrie made sure to pass on her website information too.

"I know some decorators in other cities that would love your work. I'll be happy to pass this on to them."

The big sale made December Carrie's best month yet, and she was excited to put money into her grad school account and still have enough left over for Christmas gifts.

CHAPTER 28

It's just a dream. It's just a dream. But the pounding on the door seemed so real. Don couldn't possibly be there. More pounding! Slowly, Carrie woke up and realized there really was someone pounding at the door. Her alarm clock said it was 1:16 am.

She quickly made her way downstairs and grabbed her phone. Six missed calls from Lauren and a bunch of texts. Quickly she ran over and opened the door. Lauren was standing there with the stroller, tears pouring down her face.

"Oh my gosh, come in. What's wrong?"

"It's Dustin," Lauren gasped. "He's had an overdose. The hospital called. It's bad. I have to go to him. Can you take Brittany?"

"Yes, of course. But come in for a minute." Carrie had to almost physically pull Lauren and the stroller into the house and close the door behind her. "OK, which hospital is he in?"

"He's here. He came home yesterday and was so happy. He was just going to go out with his buddies for a few hours. He didn't mean to, I know he didn't!"

"Alright, let's get a taxi to take you to the hospital. I'll keep Brittany for as long as you need, you just focus on Dustin." Carrie had to look up a taxi company on her phone before calling, but they agreed to have someone there in less than ten minutes. "OK, do you have any cash on you?"

"Yeah, I still got the money you paid me before."

"And what do I need for Brittany? How often does she eat?"

"Um, shit. Sorry. I can't think."

"It's OK, just take a couple of breaths and give yourself a minute."

Carrie watched Lauren take a few shaky breaths before she answered. "Maybe six ounces at breakfast, lunch, and supper, with some top ups in between. Oh, and a bottle before bed, too. The formula seems to be going over OK, but I don't even know if I packed everything."

"No problem. Are you OK to give me your house keys so I can pop over there if I need anything?"

"Yeah, yeah, of course. Here."

"Where's her car seat? I should probably have that, just in case."

"Oh, uh… We don't actually have a car seat. I was gonna get one soon, I promise."

"It's OK. We'll stick close to home anyways. Oh, that's the taxi." Carrie gave Lauren a big hug, and held on for a moment. "Hang in there hon, OK? Remember that we all love you and Dustin, and we're hoping for the best."

The tears flowed down Lauren's face as she hugged her back. "Thanks," she whispered before going out and running down the path to the waiting taxi.

Carrie said a heartfelt prayer for the little family before turning her attention to Brittany. She looked lost and confused. "Hey baby girl. Don't you worry. Aunty Carrie's gonna take good care of you. And just wait until Matthew and Katie wake up to find you here. You're going to make them the happiest kids on the block!"

Brittany gave Carrie a half smile before starting to fall back asleep. After checking that her diaper didn't need attention, Carrie carried her and the diaper bag upstairs. She laid her down on the safest corner of her bed and rolled up a blanket to create a barrier between them before laying down herself.

The sound of her alarm shocked both of them awake, and Brittany announced her presence in the house with a full-on wail. Matthew and Katie both came running.

"Mommy! Did you have a baby last night?" Katie's eyes were huge with shock—and hope, if Carrie wasn't mistaken. She was trying to soothe Brittany with no success.

"No silly," Matthew corrected her. "Mommy's can't have babies unless there's a daddy and she gets a giant tummy first."

"Oh." Katie's face fell.

"It's Brittany." Carrie explained over the continued screams. "Her daddy got really sick last night, so we're going to take care of her for a while so Lauren can be at the hospital."

"Is he going to die?" Katie's eyes were huge again.

"I hope not Katie-girl. I hope not... Hey, can you guys try and get ready on your own while I get a bottle ready for Brittany? And I think today calls for cereal for breakfast. Matthew, you're in charge of pouring and milk."

The kids scrambled to get ready so they could enjoy a rare weekday breakfast treat. Normally, cereal was saved for the weekends and they ate homemade oatmeal on the weekdays.

After struggling to change the furious baby, Carrie brought her downstairs along with the diaper bag. She'd never made formula before, so Brittany had to wait even longer than usual while Carrie tried to concentrate on reading the instructions. Finally she was able to sit in her favorite chair and plug the screaming mouth with the bottle.

It took a while for Brittany to calm down. Her face remained beet red, and every few seconds she took a shuddering breath as she recovered from the injustice of being woken up in a strange place by an alarm clock. The crying almost started up again when Carrie stopped to burp her, but Matthew came over and distracted her with silly faces until she forgot about crying.

"Katie, can you bring me my phone please?"

Carrie sighed in relief to see a text from Lauren saying Dustin had made it through the night and was being admitted. She couldn't imagine how hard the night had been for them. She sent a quick text saying Brittany had slept well, and was enjoying breakfast.

Then, she selected her closest friends and sent a group text:

> *Hi everyone. Lauren (the young woman who moved into our old house and does frames for me) dropped off her four-month-old baby here last night because her husband was rushed to the hospital with a very serious problem. They're really having a hard time financially, and don't have a car seat. Can anyone help out? I'd go get one myself but I have no way of getting to the store with a baby and no car seat.*

After being fed and cuddled, Brittany was content to sit propped up on Carrie's chair protected by cushions while Carrie got the kids ready to go to school. At the last minute she bundled Brittany into her snowsuit for the walk to school.

Jenny's husband Max met them at the school, as well as Kara. They both stopped to say hello to the new little star of their group before all the kids reluctantly said good-bye to Brittany and went in to school.

"Jenny's saved all of Angela's baby clothes so I'll bring some over once we find them." Max promised. "We didn't keep the car seat, though. Figured there would be something safer out there for the next baby."

It was the first Carrie heard of them thinking about growing their family. She'd definitely be talking to Jenny about that next Tuesday!

"That's OK," Kara stepped in, "I've got everything still. Maybe now I can finally let some of it go. But I only had time to grab the car seat and a bouncy chair. They're in the car."

"Oh, thank you so much! I'll probably need to pop over to their house to pick up some things. And I want to bring Brittany to the hospital for a visit."

"What happened to the dad?"

"Um, it's sensitive..." Carrie looked at Max and Kara. She knew Kara was matter-of-fact about all sorts of challenges her patients went through, and always took a solutions-based approach. And if Max was anything like his older brother Jonathan, he'd be kind no matter what. Taking a big breath, and looking at the innocent baby laying in the stroller gazing up at them all, she decided it wasn't a secret she wanted to keep.

"He had a drug overdose. I just found out last week that he's an addict. I do know that he loves Lauren and Brittany. Which is all that matters, right?" She watched them both carefully, but only saw compassion in their eyes.

"Oh man, that's so hard. I'm seeing more patients coming in with addictions and it's just devastating. For them *and* their families."

"I don't know anything about addictions, but if they've got you in their corner then they've got the best chance of getting through this."

"Thanks Max. I'll do what I can. And maybe if we can all help out with some tangible things it will ease the pressure on them..." She turned to Kara. "Can you drop the stuff off at the house? I don't think I can carry it with the stroller."

"Yeah, of course. And I should have time over the weekend to get more stuff together. Lord knows the baby ship has sailed from our house, so I really don't need to keep those things anymore!"

They all turned to go their own ways, and Carrie got lost in her thoughts. She really hadn't thought about having more kids. Becoming a mom was definitely the best thing that had ever happened to her. Did that mean she wanted to have more kids? With someone like Jonathan…?

When she got home she had to juggle the stroller with the baby gear Kara had left on her front porch. Finally inside, she unbundled Brittany and sat at the table with her while she checked her messages.

Along with another frame order, Lauren had texted to ask if Carrie could watch Brittany until tomorrow. She was going to take a taxi to pick up Dustin's truck and then go home to get some things and get a bit of sleep.

Hey there! Yes, of course I'll watch Brittany. One of my friends dropped off a car seat she doesn't use anymore. What if I came to the hospital with Brittany, and then I could drive you to Dustin's truck? Maybe seeing Brittany would help him?

CHAPTER 29

Lauren's reply later that morning made Carrie's heart sink:

ya, he's in a coma. brittany should be here. just in case. thx.

Carrie promised to be there in an hour, but was surprised by a knock at the door. Opening it, she found Jonathan standing there with two coffees and a box from the bakery down the street. Her response at his thoughtfulness was to burst into tears. Quickly he came in and put the things down before gently wrapping his arms around Carrie and Brittany.

After a minute she was able to calm down and wipe away her tears.

"I saw your text and thought you might need some coffee and food this morning. Hope it's OK to just drop in." He put the things on the table and turned to Brittany. "Do you think she'll like me?"

"Only one way to see..." Carrie set the baby into his arms and stepped back. "Meet Brittany, Brittany this is Jonathan." The two of them eyed each other for a few seconds before Jonathan smiled and was rewarded with a heart-melting smile back.

"Oh man. I haven't held anyone this tiny since Angela was born. She's perfect!"

Arms free, Carrie immediately grabbed a coffee and started opening the pastry box. "Does it matter what I take?"

Without breaking eye contact with the baby in his arms he shook his head no. "We take our coffee the same, and I got a few things from the bakery for you to choose from."

Carrie ignored the healthy-looking muffin and took out a chocolate-glazed donut. She didn't say anything until she finished the coffee. "OK, I think that was the best breakfast I've ever had. Thank you a thousand times. My alarm clock this morning freaked Brittany out, and between trying to get her calmed down and getting the kids ready I didn't have time for anything else."

"Have you heard anything more?"

"Yeah. Lauren says Dustin is in a coma. I'm going to bring Brittany to the hospital pretty quick here so she can see her daddy, and then I'll drive Lauren to wherever Dustin left the truck last night."

"What happened?" As soon as Brittany started to wiggle he started walking back and forth. She settled down to look at the new face above her again.

"Drug overdose." Jonathan looked up at her sharply. "Lauren thinks it was accidental, and I have to agree with her from what I know of him. He loves them both so much. Maybe he just got a bad bunch. I don't know. Addiction is so hard to understand and help."

"Then you're the perfect person to be there for them right now. I know you'll help."

Carrie sighed and found a few tears running down her cheeks again. She wiped them away before talking. "I hope so. But it doesn't sound good. I should change her and get a bottle ready before we leave."

"Can I come with you? I can even wait in the car, but that way you're not alone with a baby."

"Um, yeah actually. I was a bit nervous, not knowing where the truck might be parked."

After getting a bottle ready and changing Brittany's diaper they were ready to go. Jonathan came in as far as the hospital lobby and told Carrie he'd wait there for her. It took a while to find out where to go, but soon Carrie was wheeling the stroller into the ICU. She headed for the nursing desk and one of the nurses pointed to a darkened room in the corner of the ward. It looked like there was only one patient there who would be getting a visit from a baby.

Carrie tried to ignore the beeps and intercom announcements that seemed to be going off continuously as she walked over to the room. The door was open a little bit. Lauren was on the edge of a chair, her head laying on the bed beside Dustin's motionless hand. There were tubes going into his arm, wires coming out from under the covers, and a respirator was making a steady inhale and exhale as it kept him alive.

"Hey hon," she whispered.

Lauren lifted her head and looked around for a minute before focusing on Carrie and the stroller. "Hey..." She stood up and lifted Brittany out of the stroller, kissing her forehead and murmuring to her before turning to Carrie. "I missed her so much. Thank you."

She turned back to Dustin. "Hey you, look who came to visit her daddy. She misses you. You need to get better babe." Adjusting his arm a bit, she lay Brittany down beside him.

Carrie walked over and put her arm around Lauren for a minute. "There's a bottle in the bag if you need it. Take your time. I'll meet you in the lobby whenever, OK?"

Lauren nodded and Carrie quietly left the room. At the nursing station a nurse waived her over. "You're with the overdose?"

"I'm friends with Lauren and Dustin, yes." Immediately she disliked the nurse but tried to hide it and stay on her good side.

"And you've got the baby right now?"

"Yes, Lauren and I are friends, and she works for me. It's an honor to watch Brittany for them. They're such a beautiful little family. I hope he's OK. But in the meantime myself and all of our friends will help out in any way they need. We can't give the amazing medical care that you're providing. But we'll do everything else." Carrie forced herself to smile while she looked the nurse in the eye.

"Well, yes, of course. We'll do our best. It's good to know they have responsible friends…"

"I'm going to give them some time together, but I'll be waiting downstairs if they need anything. Can I bring you a coffee or a tea or anything? This must be such a challenging job up here."

"Oh, no. That's OK."

Carrie sensed a little bit of softening from the nurse. She hoped they hadn't given Lauren any trouble through the night.

Seeing Jonathan sitting in the lobby a few minutes later instantly made Carrie feel a little better. "Hey."

"Hey back. How are they?"

"I don't know. I thought they needed some time alone together so I told Lauren I'd wait for her down here. Lauren had Brittany laying in her dad's arms. It's so, so sad. And the one nurse I talked to seemed pretty biased against them. We may need to start a kindness campaign up there."

"A kindness campaign?"

"Yeah, you know. When you need to help someone remember that most people are good? Next time I come I'll bring something from that bakery for all the nurses. I hope she didn't mean to come across the way she did—as if they were scum or something. But she definitely started to change her tune when I told her that Brittany and Dustin had lots of friends who were supporting them right now."

It was nice to sit with Jonathan. He always came across as calm and level-headed. Carrie hadn't seen him in a crisis yet, but figured he could probably handle himself without losing it. She turned slightly to look at him. He was leaning forward with his elbows on his knees, his hands clasped in front of him with the knuckles turning white.

Without realizing what she was doing Carrie put a hand on his shoulder. "Um, Jonathan? You OK?"

He released his hands and rubbed the back of his neck before sitting back and looking at Carrie. She was blown away by the pain on his face.

"It's been a while since I've been in a hospital. Brings back some memories…"

Carrie moved her hand down to his arm and squeezed while shifting more so she could face him. She waited while he struggled to decide what to say.

"First it was my parents. I had to…um…identify them. You know, after…"

She felt her chest constrict with pain. Her own memories of her mom's accident were balanced with the fact that she had survived and was still alive. To lose both parents? It was too much to imagine.

"And then with Cindy…I made it to the hospital in time. But they thought the guy she was with was her fiancée so they didn't let me in right away. I figured it was just a mix up, so I pulled out my phone to show the receptionist the pictures from our engagement party and she let me in. There was this other nurse who sat with me after… and explained what they knew. Thank God I had a warning before the press got word of it. He was some big shot lawyer, so it was in the papers for days."

He took a shuddering breath and dragged a hand over his face. "Sorry. Not the stories you need to hear today. I'm here for you. You know, today."

"Thanks for telling me. I guess it's not something you talk about very often."

"No. Never. It's gotten easier though." He turned to Carrie and gave her a soft smile. "Since I moved back here. Something in the water maybe?"

She smiled back, "Maybe."

They sat side by side, each lost in thoughts but feeling comforted by being together.

"Hey Carrie…"

The sound of Lauren's voice brought Carrie back to the current situation. She stood up and looked at Lauren. Her hair was pulled back in a messy ponytail and her baggy brown t-shirt and black sweatpants hung on her thin frame. The dark circles under her eyes were even more pronounced.

"Hey…" She reached out and gently hugged Lauren, holding her until she felt her start to let go. "I brought a friend along in case he can help with the truck. This is Jonathan."

Jonathan stood up and reached out his hand to her, "I'm so sorry about your husband. If there's any way I can help, I will."

Awkwardly she shook his hand, "Yeah, thanks." After taking a minute to bundle Brittany back into her snowsuit they all walked out to the parking lot. Jonathan offered to put the stroller away while Carrie helped Lauren buckle Brittany into the car seat. She was just explaining that Jenny and Kara had a bunch of baby stuff they were happy to pass on, when Jonathan opened the door and popped his head in.

"It's possible that I lack the intelligence to actually make the stroller fold down." He looked at Lauren sheepishly, "Could you help a failure out?"

"Oh my god…" she started, but Carrie could see the hint of a smile at the corners of her mouth. A minute later they were all back in the car, and Lauren gave Carrie instructions for where she thought the truck might be. For the entire drive Jonathan kept mumbling about 'can't believe I couldn't figure it out' while Carrie and Lauren teased him.

When they finally located the truck, Carrie pulled up behind it and turned to look at Lauren. Her face paled. "I can't—"

"—Why don't I drive the truck? Then you can stay in the warm car with Brittany."

Lauren looked up at Jonathan. "You'd do that? It's not…it's not easy to drive."

"Excellent. Maybe I'll recover a bit of my lost manhood after the whole stroller thing."

With a smile Lauren passed him the keys and then slumped back against the seat. Shortly after, as Carrie was leading the way back to the townhouse, Lauren fell asleep in the passenger seat. Thank goodness Jonathan had been there so she didn't have to drive.

CHAPTER 30

A weekend with a surprise baby brought Carrie's studying to a near standstill. And nightmares layered with a four month old's sleep schedule left her completely exhausted. More than once she reminded herself—and the kids—that their challenges were small compared to what Lauren and Dustin were going through.

Lauren was able to stop by each day to spend some time with Brittany and update Carrie. Dustin's coma was medically induced to allow his brain time to recover after the overdose. There was no way to know what the prognosis was until they brought him out of the coma. Lauren was hoping that he would be fine, but Carrie's research as she tried to understand for herself what was happening wasn't hopeful.

She tried to support her friend as much as possible without discouraging her. If things were bad, then they'd be bad. Hearing about that now wouldn't help. In the meantime, everyone had rallied behind the little family.

Kara's husband Ken delivered a van load of baby gear to the townhouse and stayed to set up a crib and change table in the baby's room. They even had a standing play rocker that Brittany would love in a few more months. Beautiful baby clothes that Angela had outgrown were in the closet and on the shelf of the change table.

When Jonathan heard from Ken that the couple was sleeping on the floor, he brought over some of the furniture that he had stored in his garage. Carrie was curious about why he had it, but was too busy juggling kids, a baby, and letting her friends into the townhouse to have time to ask him about it.

Lisa and her mom filled the fridge with groceries and set a flowering plant beside the front door, and Carla offered to clean the townhouse for them if Carrie thought they would want that type of help.

By Sunday afternoon, the townhouse was ready for whatever might come next. The nursery was furnished, the main bedroom had a double bed and two night tables, the living room had a small couch, the TV was on another night table, and the kitchen had food for a few days.

Lauren was ready to spend a night at home, so Carrie invited her over for dinner first. Several times she almost fell asleep at the table, but it was good to see her take seconds of the soup and cheese biscuits that Katie had helped her make. They had made a cake for dessert, but Carrie decided it was more important to get Lauren and Brittany safely home so they could get some sleep.

After moving the car seat to the truck, Carrie drove behind Lauren to the house.

As they walked to the front door of the townhouse, Carrie tried to prepare Lauren. "So, I'm really fortunate to have some great friends, and they've all been thinking about you this weekend," she began.

"I know. The car seat is going to be great. Thank you."

"Well, there's a bit more than a car seat. I hope that's OK..." Carrie took the car seat from Lauren so she could unlock the door.

"Holy shit!" Lauren suddenly went from colorful language to speech-less. Carrie stood behind her with the kids. Katie was giggling and jumping up and down—she had just found out about the surprise on the drive over and she was thrilled.

"Lookit Lauren, your house is *way* more beautifuller than when we lived here! All you need is some of Mommy's frames!"

The innocent honesty cracked through the excitement and made Lauren finally let out the breath she had been holding. "No kidding Katie! I can't even believe all this! Oh man, I can't wait to show Dustin…" The reality of her situation hit her, and the excitement turned to tears.

Carrie put down the car seat inside and turned to comfort her friend, "Hey, we're all hoping for the best here. Soon Dustin will be back home and you can show him all this. There's more upstairs if you're interested."

Sniffing, Lauren brushed away the tears, "Yeah, let's see."

Carrie had to hold back Katie who almost raced ahead of Lauren. "Let her go first Katie, it's her home remember." She crouched to release Brittany from the car seat and bring her along to see all the excitement.

"No way! Oh my gosh, you rock! Dustin is going to flip out when he doesn't have to sleep on the floor any more. This rocks." She turned to Carrie who was just coming up the stairs, "I can't even believe this. Are you sure nobody needed it all? There's like a whole house here!"

"Yep, the baby stuff needed a good home. And for some reason Jonathan had a bunch of furniture in his garage he didn't need. I keep forgetting to ask him about that. But it's all yours now! Alright kids, let's get going. Lauren is in serious need of a good night's sleep."

"Do you want me to do more frames tomorrow? I don't want to get behind."

Carrie paused, trying to figure out what the best answer was. "I don't know. Let's just play it by ear. You've got your hands full right now."

"OK. Thanks again for everything. I mean it."

Back at home Carrie got the dessert that they hadn't yet eaten out of the fridge and she and the kids enjoyed a few minutes of quiet together. It had been fun to have a baby in the house, but she was grateful to be back to just the three of them now.

"I need us all to tidy up and get ready for school tomorrow. And then I have some serious studying to catch up on, OK?"

Soon after, Carrie was at the table with a coffee while the kids watched a DVD. She'd need to pull some late nights and early mornings if she wanted to finish the semester before Christmas.

Despite being tired, she smiled at the thought of taking two full weeks off at Christmas. She'd finally see her little sister Jessica for the first time in a year and she could hardly wait.

CHAPTER 31

"Here's to holidays!" Carrie reached around and touched glasses with the ladies around her table. It was the first official Friday night of the holidays, and she had invited everyone over for appetizers and drinks before they all went their separate ways for Christmas.

She looked at Jenny out of the corner of her eye. Yep, only the tiniest of sips and then she switched back to the sparkling juice she had brought. Carrie was delighted that her friend was either trying to get pregnant, or already holding a wonderful secret. Hopefully they'd all know soon.

Kara was holding Brittany, "Why are little girls so completely perfect? I swear Lauren, if my boys didn't take up every ounce of energy I have, she would make me want to try one more time…"

Lauren was looking more relaxed than Carrie had seen her since the overdose. Dustin had moderate brain damage. His speech was still an issue, and his right side was not responding well, but he was working tirelessly to be able to navigate stairs so he could be home for Christmas. It was looking promising that they'd spend Christmas together. The weekend before, Carrie had followed Lauren to the Christmas tree farm and they had each picked out a tree. Having a friend with a truck definitely had its perks, and Lauren was loving having the freedom to drive places now that she had a car seat.

On the other side of Lauren sat Carla, Lisa, and, Lisa's mom Maria. Amy, the other woman who lived in their house, had planned on coming tonight too, but had been whisked away for a surprise weekend by her boyfriend Jesse. He had some connection with Lisa and Maria that Carrie had forgotten, but they were all hopeful that a proposal was in the works for the weekend.

"What do you think Amy's mom will say if she gets engaged?"

"Well, considering Amy's likely to get married before she gets pregnant, and Jesse actually has a house they'll be in when they start a family, I expect her to be pretty excited," Lisa grinned. "Having her other daughter and grandson living in her apartment isn't exactly working out."

Maria piped up, "Jesse's a darling boy. I hope they do get married." She looked pointedly at Lisa, "I'll celebrate *any* wedding I can find these days."

Lisa ignored her mom and turned to Carrie, "How's the business going?"

"Fantastic! Having Lauren's artistic eye has been priceless. We're trying all sorts of new frames and finishes, and they're selling really well. Oh, did I tell you I have a website?"

"No! You need to get better about blowing your own horn!" The women who didn't know about Carrie's website all entered it onto their phones, and soon they were sharing posts of their favorites on Facebook, Instagram, and Pinterest. Carrie tried to keep track of who liked what. Some preferred the colorful ones, and others appreciated the more classic looks. She'd love nothing more than to give all her friends something as a thank you for being so supportive.

The talk turned to Christmas plans. Lisa and Maria were heading to Mexico for a week. Carrie noticed that while Maria looked happy, the physical symptoms of her rheumatoid arthritis were becoming more obvious. She was glad they could still travel.

Jenny, Max, Angela, and Jonathan were all flying to Jenny's parent's place for a week. Her parents claimed both Max and Jonathan as their own sons and were thrilled to have everyone for the holidays.

"Chris will really miss Jonathan," Carla added. "Those two are like little kids together with all their plans!"

Carrie was dying of curiosity. She knew Jonathan had been really busy lately, but he had said it was work, so she hadn't pried. He *had* asked if she minded getting a babysitter so he could take her out for a few hours on Sunday afternoon before they went skating with the kids. Maybe then he'd tell her more.

Hours later nearly all the food was gone, and the ladies had talked and laughed to their hearts content. Even with such different stories and backgrounds, the experience of being a woman was universally fantastic and frustrating. But all of them seemed so happy to do their thing. They agreed that it was refreshing to hang out together.

The evening was declared a success, and they started to say their good-byes. Kara and Ken had invited everyone to spend New Year's at their house again, and Carrie knew her kids were already talking about it.

On Saturday Lauren and Carrie were going to go to the thrift stores. Carrie wasn't worried about inventory—her dad promised a whole 'new' batch of frames was waiting for her—but Lauren wanted to see how Carrie picked things out, in case she had time to do more looking over Christmas.

The more frames Lauren did, the more her confidence grew. Carrie knew that having a chance to be in control of your earnings was incredibly empowering, especially when the realities of poverty were still so fresh. And despite the challenges that were facing her when Dustin came home, she was so grateful he was alive that everything else took a backseat.

At the thrift stores, the women left Matthew in charge of Brittany in the stroller while they looked through the household items. Carrie found some frames that had interesting shapes, and then they went to look for fabrics that might be good for framing. So far Carrie had used women's scarves, a vintage corduroy suit jacket, a quilt, and some skirts. This time she found some fantastic vintage curtains that had a texture to them that Carrie just couldn't stop running her fingers over. By the time they were cut to size and put into frames you wouldn't be able to tell what their original purpose was.

While Carrie was waiting in line at the checkout, Lauren wandered back through the store. When Carrie found her again, she was crouched by a stack of paintings leaning against the wall near the back storage room.

"What did you find?"

"Well, a few of these paintings, they're kinda crap, but they have potential, you know?"

Carrie looked at the paintings. They were all old landscapes. Nothing at all worth putting on the wall as far as she was concerned. "Nope, sorry, I don't see it."

"I think I can make them better. I'm gonna try. I'll pay for them, in case it doesn't work."

"Yeah, of course. I totally trust your eye, I guess I'm just not seeing what you're seeing."

A short while later they were loading up their purchases and saying goodbye. Carrie was heading to her parent's house tomorrow afternoon. She wished she could be around for Dustin's homecoming, but she had agreed to pick her sister up from the airport on the way to her parents.

"Let me know how things go with Dustin and everything, OK? And we'll be back in just over a week. I can't wait to see what you do with those paintings!"

"Don't get your hopes up!" She let each of them give Brittany a hug goodbye before buckling her in the car seat. "You kids have fun this week, and come back soon so Brittany doesn't forget you."

"Lauren? Thanks so much for all your help with the business."

Lauren shrugged. "What else would I do? Maybe by the time you're back everything will be sold!" While Carrie was out of town Lauren would take care of shipping if there were any sales. Since it was the first year of having a website, Carrie didn't know whether people would buy in the week before Christmas.

The next day Jonathan drove over in the afternoon to pick Carrie up. Walking down the stairs she heard Katie stage whisper to Jonathan.

"Uncle Johnny, are you taking Mommy on a date?"

"I am, but don't tell your Mommy, 'kay? We'll let her think we're just hanging out."

Carrie stepped into the room trying to hide her smile. "What are you two whispering about?"

Wide eyed with false innocence, Katie replied, "Nothing Mommy. We're *not* having secrets."

"OK. You two be good. We'll be back in time for skating." Carrie made sure the babysitter was set and then she followed Jonathan to the car. As usual, he was looking good in fitted jeans, a green waffle knit henley, and his brown leather jacket.

Carrie was getting another year's use out of her tall brown boots and had paired them with stretch jeans, a bright yellow sweater, and a white scarf. Her black winter coat didn't exactly add to the outfit, but she'd be warm enough to take it off when they were skating later.

"So…" Jonathan began once they got in the car. He looked nervous. Carrie couldn't imagine what was going on.

"So... well... a few months ago you said something that really made me re-evaluate pretty much everything."

He started the car and began driving. "You were talking about finishing grad school without going into debt and how important that was to you. And it really got me to thinking. Until that point I didn't really care about debt because it's been pretty easy for me to keep up with my bills. But then here you are, being super careful about everything you spend, just to make sure you don't get into debt. And I decided that I wanted to do the same thing – get rid of my debt and start saving for a... um, well... for the future."

He pulled the car over a few blocks later and turned to look at Carrie. "I'm not telling you this to brag. It's important for me to be honest with you about where I'm at. I found some new clients and have some pretty nice contracts going right now. I'm putting every-thing extra I make into paying off my own student loans."

"Seriously? That's fantastic!" Although Carrie was thrilled to know she had made a good impression on him, she still didn't know why he needed to drive her down the road to tell her all this.

"But I thought I could do more. So... I partnered up with Chris to flip this house." He gestured to the house near them with the 'For Sale' sign in front of it. "This is the finished product."

"You bought a house?" It was easily the nicest house on the block — and that was saying a lot, because this was one of the nicer neighbor-hoods in the area. The two story house had a welcoming porch with a bright red front door, and black trim set against white siding. Even from the car Carrie could see that the blinds inside were high end.

"This is what it looked like two months ago." He pulled out his phone and Carrie leaned over to look. It didn't even look like the same house! "Come on, I'll show you!"

The house was better than a show home — or at least what she thought a show home would look like. It was perfect, and she told him so.

"This is really fantastic! Now I get what you've been so busy with lately. And does this have anything to do with all that furniture in your garage?"

"Yeah, there were some really great things left here by the previous owner. I'm sorry. The plan was to pass that furniture onto you, but I was waiting because I knew you'd ask where it came from, and I didn't want to tell you about my plan until I knew it would work! Plus, the house was a mess to start and I didn't want to scare you away by showing it to you before we were done. And then when you told me about Lauren and Dustin, I just thought I had to give it to them."

"I totally agree. That was such a big part of setting them up to be ready for Dustin to come home. And if this is what you and Chris can do with a place, you're well on your way." Carrie tried to look at the house as it was now, comparing it with his 'before' picture. "So, you must have been doing work here too. There's no way Chris could have done it all with his other jobs."

"Yup, I had to reintroduce myself to manual labour! But it was worth it. I covered the costs for this one. After we sell the house we'll take some of the profits to do it again, and split the rest. If it meets our target, then it will be a big part of Chris and Carla putting the past behind them. And if we can pull off a couple more of these, he'll be able to start his business again and I'll have my mortgage paid off. See what you've done?"

"Pardon? I'm not the one who busted a gut to fix up this house! You and Chris deserve all the credit."

"Carrie, this whole thing wouldn't have even occurred to me without you. And Chris wasn't in a financial position for a project like this, so he couldn't have done it himself for another few years. It was the way you were so focused on getting out of debt that made me think I could do the same thing."

CHAPTER 32

Christmas morning was perfect. Carrie continued her tradition of giving her parents and sister a family photo of her and the kids, but she added individual gifts for each of them that she never could have afforded a year ago. It was so fulfilling to finally be able to do something tangible to show them how much she valued them. She and Jessica had pooled their money to buy their mom a brand new smartphone. Now they'd be able to easily video chat with her whenever they wanted!

The kids got things from their wish list from their auntie and grandparents, and a few little things from Carrie. Then, after everything had calmed down and the small mountain of wrapping paper and packaging had been dealt with, she 'remembered' one more gift and handed them each an envelope.

Katie opened hers first, and looked at the picture of a girl on a balance beam with confusion. "Is this a painting Mommy?"

"No, what's the girl doing?"

"She's doing gymnastics…" Katie looked up with wide eyes. "Do I get to do gymnastics?"

"Yep! You're going to go on Tuesdays after school and Saturday mornings." Carrie wasn't sure if it was going to work to have Matthew plus Kara's three boys with her at the gymnastics center every week, but looking at Katie's happy face she decided to make it work no matter what.

Now, Matthew was eager to open his envelope. Pulling out a picture of an electric piano, he ran over and buried Carrie in a huge hug. "Thank you Mom!"

Smiling over his shoulder at her parents, Carrie hugged him back. "You're welcome! And you'll get lessons each week too. Grandpa's got the piano downstairs. For now, you can set it up in my bedroom near where you're sleeping if you want. We'll take it home with us when we go."

Getting the piano had been the highlight of her dad's second hand shopping this year. Carrie didn't think he'd be able to find anything within her $50 budget, but he had. Fortunately, the piano teacher she found would come to the house on Wednesday evenings, so Carrie didn't have to juggle taking the kids out for another lesson.

Just before lunch they all had a video chat with Jonathan to tell him about their morning. Although her dad already knew who Jonathan was from Carrie's move in the summer, her mom hadn't met him so was happy to put a face to the name. Carrie had admitted the night before that she found herself thinking about him as more than a friend. It was the first time she said out loud what she was feeling, and immediately afterwards she felt a strange combination of relief and regret.

Her parents were supportive, without really saying anything one way or the other. Jessica, on the other hand was full-on pushing Carrie to go for it. Already she had 'casually' asked the kids a few things about Jonathan and liked what she was hearing. When Carrie moved to her bedroom with earbuds to have a bit of a private talk with him, she missed the excited conversation between her mom and sister about Jonathan definitely being a keeper.

Of course, she found out on the car ride back to her house when Katie innocently asked what a keeper was…

Driving up to her house, Carrie found herself smiling. It was a long way from the dreary townhouse that they used to call home. Now, with Christmas lights twinkling in the front windows and a clean and tidy front yard, she was proud of where they lived.

It didn't take long to unload the car with both kids helping, and they were happy to go off and play with their Christmas gifts as soon as Carrie let them. She started a load of laundry and packaged up an order that had come through yesterday before sitting on the couch to catch up on all the messages from her friends.

Jonathan: *Glad you're home safe. Can't wait to see you all! Max, Jenny, and Angela say hi. Jenny's parents do too. Hey, Chris said people are looking at the house! Might get it sold soon!*

Carla: *I'm sooooooo excited about the guys' project. Chris has been back to his old self since they got started, which is awesome. It nearly killed me to not tell you about it sooner! Too cute that Jonathan wanted it to be a surprise for you…*

Lisa sent a gorgeous update from the beach in Mexico. Her mom looked so relaxed and happy. It looked to Carrie like another big step on their healing journey.

There was nothing from Kara and Ken, but Carrie wasn't surprised. They had started a 'no phones rule' during family holidays now that Calvin and Justin both had phones. Kara reluctantly agreed with Ken that they should set the example as parents. As soon as they were back Carrie knew she'd be rapid-texting.

But most surprising was a text from Lauren asking if they wanted to come over for a pizza supper that evening. Carrie really didn't want to add more work for them, especially with Dustin just being home for a week, but she couldn't think of a way to say no. So, a few hours later they were walking to their old home. It was chilly, but they all needed some fresh air.

Lauren welcomed them in, and immediately passed Brittany off to Carrie. Dustin was sitting on the couch and looked fine.

"Hi Dustin! Good to see you!" It was only when he tried to smile and waved at them with his left hand that it was obvious he was dramatically different. The right side of his face and body barely moved. To the side of the couch was a walker.

Katie went right up and climbed on the couch. The rest of them fell silent as she reached up and gently touched the unresponsive side of his face. "You look different," she said matter-of-factly. "That's OK."

He gestured to Lauren, and she spoke up. "He's different on the outside, but still the same great guy on the inside."

"Is that why he went to the hospital for a long time?"

"Yeah. He can't really talk, and one side of his body doesn't work good, but he's already figured out how to change Brittany's diaper!"

"Wow," this from Matthew, "That's pretty cool."

Katie started up her own monologue with Dustin—she always had a lot to say and was thrilled that this adult was such a captive audience. Carrie asked him if Katie should take a break but he shook a hand 'no' and gave a half smile.

Lauren looked nervous. "OK, before the pizza comes I have something to show you."

Carrie followed her into the kitchen and stopped short. Every surface had a painting on it. They seemed to be the same sizes as the ones they had seen at the thrift store, but there's no way they could be the same ones. These paintings were gorgeous, drawing you in to scenes of cabins in the woods, deer peeking through a forest, families playing in the background, and one with a brilliant foreground of flowers in front of a muted meadow and pond.

"These…Wow! Lauren! These cannot be the same paintings! They just can't! I can't even believe how incredibly talented you are. How on earth did you pull this off?"

"I don't know. I just wanted to rescue them and give them another chance. Are you sure they're OK? I didn't spend a lot of money buying them, so it's fine if they're crap."

"Are you kidding me? These are the most amazing paintings I've ever seen. Honestly, I feel like I've just found out my friend is a secret rock star or something! What do you plan on doing with them?"

Lauren gave Carrie a blank look, "Do? They're finished. Ready to sell if you think they're good enough."

"Are you kidding? People will love these! They're like the ultimate upcycling. I mean, I can't even remember what they looked like before."

"Oh good, I thought for a minute you didn't want to sell them. Can I get the same as you pay me for the frames, plus what I paid for the pictures?"

"You did these for *my* website? Lauren, I'd be honored to sell these on my site, but there's no way I'm paying you the same as for the frames. I'll take a twenty percent commission on the sale price. Besides, you've paid for all these supplies too. That's a big deal."

A sound from the living room interrupted their conversation and it took a second for Carrie to realize it was Dustin trying to say something.

Lauren didn't seem phased by the sound and waved to Carrie to follow her out of the kitchen. Once they were standing around Dustin, she continued. "First of all, these are all my supplies. I didn't pay for anything, I just asked my mom to ship them to me as a Christmas present. Trust me, knowing I'm painting again is the best news she's heard in years."

Dustin grunted again and held up two fingers and pointed to him and Lauren.

"Dustin says *we'll* take twenty percent and I'll keep doing frames for the same rate. Carrie, we owe you so much. Please let us do this for you."

"You don't owe me anything. We're friends," she gave a wry smile, "And anyways, you can't put a price on that. But these paintings are your chance to make it big, and I'm not going to take that away from you. Not. A. Chance."

With a dramatic sigh, Dustin held up five fingers.

"Fifty-fifty?" Carrie asked.

He nodded. She turned to Lauren, who's huge smile said it all.

"OK, this just turned into an even bigger celebration dinner!" She reached out her hand to Lauren, "I will always remember the day you gave me the honor of showcasing your paintings. Thank you."

Lauren grabbed her and gave an enthusiastic high five. Katie turned to Dustin, "High five for the mommies!" He held his hand up and she gave it a good smack. Their happy fest was only interrupted by the doorbell ringing.

"Pizza's here!"

CHAPTER 33

The rest of the holiday flew by as Carrie and the kids caught up on sleeping in, spending time with their friends, and hanging out together. In between, Carrie and Lauren worked together with the lady who designed Carrie's original website to add a new section for Lauren's paintings.

They decided to title the collection *Beautiful World* and promoted it as salvaging and repurposing neglected art to make the world a little greener and more beautiful. Keeping in mind the income cap on the subsidized housing, Carrie cautioned Lauren about letting her name get too well-known before they had a chance to move. They only used Lauren's first name and the term "independent artist" on the website.

Really, the place they were in wasn't suitable for Dustin. They needed something on one level that was accessible. Lauren admitted it was scary to get him up and down the stairs, but with this new venture Carrie was confident they'd be in a position to upgrade soon. Dustin tended to side with her, but Lauren couldn't believe she'd actually be able to make a living as an artist.

Having someone else who could really benefit from the website's exposure gave Carrie a new incentive to promote it. She replaced the frames behind Jenny's desks with one of Lauren's paintings, which Jenny insisted she had to have. In turn they insisted on selling it to her for half price ($125) in exchange for Jenny showcasing the new painting whenever she had a video conference with a client.

As usual, their entire group of friends enthusiastically supported the new venture, and orders started coming in at a regular pace. In January Carrie cleared over $2,200 on top of paying Lauren $1,500. They joked about which one of them was more surprised by the big numbers, while Dustin motioned that he knew it all along.

The prognosis for Dustin was less encouraging. While he was getting better at walking around, he found trying to speak incredibly frustrating. Lauren was good at figuring out most things, but it took time. He could write a bit with his left hand, but because he was right-handed, it was hard. Lauren admitted that what upset him the most was not being able to talk to Brittany.

There was some technology that might help him, but it was really expensive. Lauren's first priority was moving to a better home. Then she'd focus on somehow helping him talk.

He was managing to do much more of Brittany's care, freeing up Lauren to continue painting, and keeping him busy. In a few weeks his parents would be coming for a visit to meet Brittany for the first time. They had never forgiven Lauren for introducing him to drugs, and no one knew how the visit would go, especially now that drugs had left their son partially paralyzed and unable to speak.

Carrie had barely seen Jonathan since he got home. Between her business and him closing the sale on the house, they had resorted to sending quick texts throughout the day. Carrie had pictured a week of doing things with him and the kids, and maybe even watching a movie or two together at night, but it just didn't work out.

Before she started her next semester, she texted him a picture of her textbooks:

See you in four months.

He replied with a crying face, and then more happy/sad news:

Aw… and it looks like Chris and I have found our next house. If we can pull this off one more time he'll be able to pay off the debts from his old business. So we're going to go for it! But it does mean I'll be pretty busy for the next while too…

It turned out to be true for both of them. Even their Sunday afternoons together with the kids had to be scaled down to once a month. In January Jonathan did manage to take Carrie out to dinner to celebrate her thirty-third birthday. They both were too tired to add a movie onto their evening, but Carrie enjoyed the huge bouquet of flowers he gave her for the rest of the week.

The extra income that Lauren's work brought to Framed made all the difference for Carrie. She finally told Jenny in February that she didn't need the cleaning job anymore.

"I don't suppose I can pay you double to just come over for our chats still? And I'm only half joking."

Carrie smiled at Jenny, "I'm going to miss them too. A lot. It's just too easy to fill my schedule with school and work and the kids, and then go for weeks without having a real conversation with another woman. Now that Kara has the boys in rugby she's always rushing when she picks them up from my place. Pretty soon they'll be jumping in the open van door as she drives by!"

"And? What about the business?" Ever since Carrie had confided her fears about finances to Jenny she had taken a personal stake in Carrie's success. While she had been unsure about Carrie's decision to include Lauren in such a big way, it was clearly paying off.

"You're not going to believe it!"

"Try me."

"OK…so remember in January I paid Lauren fifteen hundred and cleared over two thousand on top of that?" Jenny nodded. "Well, we're already past that, and the month isn't even finished!"

"You're wrong—I do believe it! But only because I keep looking at your website and wanting everything. So this is a big change for both of you. How are you coping?"

"For now, I'm just putting almost everything extra into the grad school account. That helps me keep my feet on the ground. But I think that Lauren's feeling a bit overwhelmed with the money. Remember, last summer they were homeless until I moved out and they moved into the townhouse? Do you think you could sit down with her and give her some advice? Like what you did with me?"

"Definitely! I'm so happy you're doing OK now, but there was something special when you started out, and I *do* miss those types of interactions. Here, I'll text you the times I have free next week, and you can set something up with her. It can be here, or your house, or Lauren's house. Wherever she feels comfortable."

"Thanks Jenny, you're the best! Now, I'm happy to stay on here for as long as you need until you can find another housecleaner."

"Carrie! You've got enough on your plate. I can find any old housecleaner in no time. It's just you that I'll never be able to replace. So today's your last day."

Carrie did her best to do extra for Jenny, but the time went way too fast. It felt strange to be closing the door on a source of income, but she knew the extra study time would really help her keep up. When she popped her head into Jenny's office to wave goodbye, she felt herself getting emotional. Jenny had been a lifeline to her when she needed one the most.

CHAPTER 34

Carrie sat at the kitchen table with her laptop in front of her. She was about to hit 'send' on the last paper of the year. With her hand hovering above the enter key, she looked around her. In the middle of a late night study session a few weeks ago she got the crazy idea to have a party when she sent the last paper in. Now, all of her friends were standing around the table in complete silence just waiting for her to hit that key.

"You do realize that after this you'll all be stuck with me for four months. Phone calls, texts, visits, you'll never get rid of me!"

"Bring it on babe!" Lauren shouted back.

As soon as she hit send, Jonathan and Max both popped the corks on bottles of prosecco, and the kids broke open some party poppers that sent streamers flying through the air. Eight-month-old Brittany squealed in delight over all the colors.

Carrie quickly put her laptop away and accepted a glass from Jonathan. "To Carrie!" he shouted, and everyone replied. Even though she was exhausted, already the stress and challenges of the school year were fading. Her business was exceeding her expectations, she'd be able to pay for her second year of grad school, her kids were happy and healthy, Jonathan was done flipping houses for now, Jenny was healthy, Dustin and Lauren had moved into an accessible three-bedroom apartment where she had set up her own studio…what more could she ask for?

Everyone helped set out the food they brought. Carrie's invitation had clearly stated they were to bring everything needed for a party. A year ago she never would have sent such a request. But now she was surrounded by people who would always help out when she needed them, even if all she needed from them was a party.

By the end of the evening Carrie was beyond exhausted, but so happy. She really couldn't care less what her worried self might tell her during her next quiet moment. The facts spoke for themselves. Everything was going to be OK. One year from now she'd be getting ready to start her six-month internship and then she could apply to be a registered counseling psychologist. For the first time she was starting to believe that her dream could become a reality, and not just stay a dream for the rest of her life.

The next morning Carrie almost ignored her alarm and went back to sleep. It was only Katie coming in for morning cuddles and excited chatter about going to gymnastics that forced her to get up. Even Matthew was still sleeping after the late night. "OK Katie-girl. How about I get you some breakfast and put on a DVD for you while I shower?"

Katie tore down the stairs and Carrie followed, struggling to put one foot in front of the other. Thank goodness she didn't have any studying or papers to write, because there's no way her brain could do any work this morning!

After coffee, gymnastics, coffee, and grocery shopping Carrie came home to her post-party house. It wasn't that bad, just not her usual tidy house. By this time Matthew was begging her to take in the cans and bottles that had been stacking up in the back yard for months. Since he got the majority of the cash for the returns there was always a big incentive for him. The last thing Carrie wanted to do was go out again, but the guilt for focusing on school for the last few months compelled her to agree. "But only after we clean up the house. Matthew, you bring up the stuff from the basement where you guys were playing last night. And Katie, you clean up your room from all the stuff you, Magnus, and Angela did last night. *Then* we'll go to the recycling depot."

"And can I go buy candy after, Mommy?"

"Yes, but only a little bit!"

"Yay!" Katie ran upstairs and Carrie looked at her longingly. She either wanted her energy, or half an hour upstairs in her bed…

On the way home Carrie decided to go through the McDonald's drive through. There was no way she was cooking tonight. While they were waiting for their order, Matthew asked if they could go to church tomorrow. They hadn't been since Easter—Carrie had found that sleeping in on Sundays was more important.

"Yeah, I guess we can go."

"And can you tell everyone else? I like it when we're all there together."

Carrie agreed and sent out a group text when they got home. She struggled to stay awake until it was Matthew's bedtime and then gladly followed him. Her mattress on the floor had never felt so good, but as she fell asleep she wondered if she could finally afford a proper bed. Sometime soon she needed to get caught up on tracking her finances. It was another thing that had been put aside in the past few months.

The next morning Katie came downstairs in a dress that she had clearly outgrown. She was adamant about wearing it, and Carrie finally found a pair of pink shorts to put underneath, so at least it was decent. And when Matthew came down she noticed that his pants were sitting well above his ankles. When did this happen? She couldn't believe she hadn't noticed they had grown out of all their clothes. But when she went to get dressed herself, she had to admit they were all long overdue for some new clothes. It would have been nice to throw on a fun skirt or dress, but Carrie was limited to jeans and the only blouse in her closet that didn't need ironing. At least she could wear sandals. That was as much 'spring' as she could do.

When they got to church Carrie recognized the same lady who had sat beside her months ago. Feeling friendly, she went into the same row and introduced herself and the kids. The woman's name was Mary and she had been going to the same church for forty years!

"Are you a grandma?" Katie asked, after positioning herself between her mom and Mary.

"Well yes, I am. But my grandsons live a long way away so I don't see them very often."

"Grandma Mary, do you like pizza?"

Carrie shared a smile with Matthew as Katie worked her magic and got into a conversation with her new friend. A short time later Jonathan joined them.

"Hey bud, thanks for the invitation this morning. It's definitely nicer to be here with you guys." He looked over Matthew's head at Carrie. "Have you caught up on sleep yet?"

"Not even close!"

When the kids went off to Sunday School Jonathan moved over until his shoulder was just close enough to brush against Carrie's every once in a while. Between wanting to sleep, and having Jonathan so close to her Carrie didn't get a single word of the sermon. Not that she was complaining.

Afterwards she left Mary chatting with Jonathan and went to pick up Katie from her class. Matthew would make his own way back to where they were sitting. Carrie recognized a few of the other parents from school and gymnastics but was too tired to do more than smile and stand a little back from the conversations.

When she got back with Katie, Jonathan and Mary had already

exchanged numbers. "Your friend here tells me you're probably too tired today, so next week I want to take you all out for lunch after the service. I'd like to continue my conversation with Katie, and get to know Matthew too!"

Carrie agreed. It seemed a little strange to have an elderly lady treating them to lunch, but as long as it wasn't today, she was fine with it. They said their goodbyes and she promised to text Jonathan when she had caught up on sleep later in the week.

CHAPTER 35

Monday morning Carrie found herself too awake to sleep past her alarm, but still very tired. She went downstairs for a first cup of coffee and decided to take a look at her budget and savings. Up until January she had tracked her finances every week but it had barely crossed her mind since. All she'd done was quickly make sure nothing unexpected came out of her account and move everything she didn't need for monthly expenses into her grad school savings account.

At first she couldn't believe her numbers. Although the website sales were doing fantastic, and Lauren and Carrie had continued to finish frames on top of Lauren's paintings, it hadn't really registered with Carrie how good she was doing. She needed $9,000 for tuition, minus the $800 bursary that she'd receive. And right now…. She logged out of her online bank account and then logged back in. Then she scrolled down through the deposits. It *looked* right…

Account Balance: $7,213.79

"No way," she breathed. And then, as if to confirm the universe really was on her side, an email popped up with another sale from

185

her website. In disbelief, Carrie went through the motions of packing up the two paintings that had been purchased, and booking the courier company to collect them in the afternoon.

When the kids got up, she made oatmeal, checked their lunches, and walked them to school without really registering what was going on. Back at home she checked over everything again. Somehow she had gotten so caught up with the day-to-day of studying, painting frames, and listing things on the website that she hadn't noticed how fast her account was growing!

Did this change everything? Definitely. It wasn't just that the pressure of paying her tuition was almost gone. It was that she really only needed to cover her expenses when school started again. And even if sales slowed down, she could easily do that. Easily!

Realizing it was laundry day, Carrie went upstairs to gather up their dirty clothes. But when she started to sort the laundry and saw the 'too small' things her kids had worn to church the day before, she changed her mind. Dropping everything she grabbed her purse and headed to the mall. Halfway there she detoured to the thrift stores first. Old habits die hard.

She did find some good kids clothes at the thrift stores, along with some paintings for Lauren to rescue and some frames. Finally certain she had done her best to bargain shop, she headed to the mall. While she was trying on jeans her phone pinged. It was Jonathan:

I came over with coffee but you're not here.

Without thinking she quickly texted back:

At the mall shopping!

Her phone rang.

"Hey Jonathan,"

"Carrie! Is everything OK?"

"Yeah…" She held up the two pairs of jeans that fit, trying to choose between them.

"Are you sure? I've never heard of you going to the mall, let alone to shop."

She lowered her voice, wondering if the sound echoed in the change-room. "You'll never believe this, but I'm way ahead of the game in my grad school account. Waaayyyy ahead. So I just decided to go shopping. And I don't even feel guilty."

"Carrie, that's fantastic! I'm so happy for you! OK, well, I guess I'll drink an extra coffee then. Have fun!"

She grabbed the jeans and a neat white t-shirt with a print of a paint-brush dripping a rainbow of paint from it and went to pay. Next stop was buying a fun summer dress, and then new underwear for herself and the kids.

Carrie just had time to start the laundry and make sandwiches for snack before picking up Katie from school. With the older boys in rugby they were always starving, so she had resorted to serving mini meals after school. Definitely the favorite was when she cooked trays of French fries, but that was a once-in-a-while treat.

After Kara and the boys left, Carrie made a tray with chicken, pota-toes, and carrots to cook in the oven for dinner. Now that she had a nice backyard and some room in her budget, she was going to get a small barbeque, but they'd have to live with oven-roasted food until then.

Just before heading to bed she checked her phone again. Another sale! Tomorrow Lauren was coming over, and Carrie would work with her to get their stock of frames back up. The website was down to just a handful of listings again. *What I really need is someone else to do frames with me so Lauren can focus on paintings.*

Her sleep was interrupted by another nightmare. If she hadn't been so tired, she might have laughed at the irony of losing sleep now, when she didn't need to get up early to study. Rolling over, she turned on a little lamp and pulled her journal out from under the bed. After a quick re-write of the nightmare she easily fell back asleep.

CHAPTER 36

"Are you sure you're OK?" Kara rarely looked worried about anything, but she was most definitely worried.

"Actually, I'm kind of relieved. The business is so intense right now that I don't think I could handle childcare on top of everything else."

Kara had invited Carrie out for coffee while they kids were at school to tell her that Ken would be taking the summer off, and they wouldn't need any childcare.

"Oh good. I really didn't want to make things harder for you. And now, if you ever need you can drop off *your* kids at *my* place!"

Carrie savored the lemon bar that Kara had insisted on buying for each of them along with their lattes. "I'm so happy for Ken and your boys. They're going to have such a great summer. Will you get any time off?"

"Yep. Now that I have a tiny bit of seniority I'll take a few days here and there. But not having to get the boys up and out the door before I get to work is going to feel like a holiday in itself! So, tell me more about the business. I saw the one painting Lauren did on the wall in your living room. Gorgeous!"

"I know. She gave it to me a few weeks after my birthday. She's so incredibly talented, and already the painting sales are totally supporting her family. It's such a perfect set-up. The only problem is that I could really use some help doing frames. I was looking back over the sales for this year, and frame sales went up at the same time as we started putting Lauren's paintings up. I don't suppose you know anyone with moderate painting skills that's looking for some extra work?"

"Not right now, but I'll keep my ears open. It's definitely a job that a variety of people can do, right? Like even those with accessibility issues?"

Carrie felt like she'd been smacked upside the head, "*What* did you say?"

"Oh, I didn't mean anything bad! It's just that someone could work on the frames sitting down, or if they had hearing loss or something. You know, it's accessible."

"Yeah, I hear you. I just can't believe I've been so incredibly dense!" Kara looked confused, so Carrie continued, "My mom! Last summer she helped me do some frames while we were staying with her and she loved it. *Why* did I not think of asking if she wanted to do more? Geez, I can't believe myself sometimes."

Kara started laughing, "Really? You've got this huge successful business and you're calling yourself dense? I don't think so Carrie. But how cool would it be to have your mom working for you?"

They finished their coffees and Carrie went home to video chat with her mom. Thank goodness she had a decent phone now! Her mom was very happy to help, but equally reluctant to accept any pay. After going back and forth, Carrie suggested they put that money into a separate account to save for a family holiday they could all take together. That would be a first for them, and something worth saving for. She knew it would take a few weeks for her mom to finish enough frames to make it worth it for her dad to bring them to her, but knowing they were being done would definitely take some of the pressure off. And with the video chat function her mom could easily get direction on frames, styles, and colors.

In the meantime Carrie was dealing with almost daily shipments, updating the website with new listings every week, continuing to finish frames, be mom to her kids, and caregiver to Kara's kids. Looking back she had no idea how she had managed to finish the semester on time without collapsing completely.

As soon as camps became available Carrie started registering her kids. She needed to be close to home for the summer to keep up with the business, and she wanted the kids to be doing more than sitting and watching TV every day.

Being able to just choose things the kids would like, instead of looking for free or discounted camps was another new, exciting experience for all of them. In addition to a week of Vacation Bible School at the church, Matthew was going away for five days of camping with the Boys' Club, and Katie was going to do a week of half-day gymnastics and another week of half-day fun sports camp. Of course, Carrie immediately regretted telling Katie about it so soon, as the 'how long until camp' questions were now part of every conversation!

The sweet grandma they had met at church was also part of their summer plans. During their lunch out together they learned that Mary had been a home economics teacher well into her sixties, and she volunteered at a drop-in center downtown once a week, teaching basic cooking skills. She loved to bake and had suggested to Carrie that the kids spend some time baking with her over the summer.

Carrie hoped that she'd be able to get enough work done when the kids were busy to have time to spend with them when they were home. She was already wondering how long she could keep up with everything on her own. It seemed like the business was becoming her boss instead of the other way around!

CHAPTER 37

July was busy, but manageable. Carrie decided that she wasn't going to lose her whole summer to the business, so she forced herself to quit every day by four and take the weekends completely off except for going to yard sales to look for more stock.

Matthew was back to helping out more with frames, and Carrie increased his pay to $10 for every frame he prepped and primed. Having his help allowed her to keep enough listings on the website, and when her dad came with a car-load of finished frames from her mom she had the luxury of setting some aside to list later. Immediately she transferred $400 to the new vacation savings account she had opened. Jessica wanted to be included too but they refused to let her put any money in until she knew for sure she could get time off to join them, even though they couldn't imagine a family vacation without her.

Now that she wasn't relying on Lauren to keep the frames going, Carrie insisted that she only focus on her paintings. Without asking, Carrie decreased her commission on paintings to 20% so that Lauren would still be able to support her family. By the time Lauren realized what she was doing, Carrie was ready to stand firm, and with Jenny's help they drafted a contract to make it official.

Carrie had also convinced their local TV station to do a short feature on Lauren's work as part of their Go Green focus. Upcycling was trending everywhere, and the response to Lauren's art was very positive. A local art gallery also offered to carry her paintings, but they were only prepared to offer her 40% commission so Carrie happily kept Lauren as her own.

The kids were enjoying their first summer where ice cream was always in the freezer, there was room for friends to come over and play, and they went fun places on the weekend like the zoo and the lake. Jonathan often joined them when they went out, and Carrie had invited everyone over for a barbeque twice already. She couldn't believe how lucky she was to have money to buy food for entertaining and was taking full advantage of it.

Thanks to their regular yard sale outings, and being able to borrow Lauren and Dustin's truck whenever she needed, the house was now comfortably furnished with an eclectic variety of things. The basement had their old small couch, another TV, bean bag chairs, and a foosball table that Carrie got for free when she arrived at a yard sale just as it started to rain.

On the main floor a bright orange vintage couch sat in front of a deep blue coffee table. Beside the couch was the plant she had rescued the very first time she ever took a piece of furniture to refinish out of a dumpster. It was loving its new home.

Although everyone teased her about her rainbow room, they quit when they sat on the couch. It was so comfortable it was getting a reputation for putting people to sleep! Carrie loved how the bright colors set off her tropical print armchair, Lauren's painting, and some of her own bright frames that had finally found their way onto her walls. Being able to do whatever she wanted in the house—and to have some money to do it—helped the wounds from her marriage to Don continue to heal. She felt like she was finally letting her real self show, and the people who knew her best liked who she was.

The last Thursday in July Carrie got a strange text from Kara:

Am on my way over with a girl who needs you.

Trusting that Kara would have told her more if she could, Carrie sent the kids out the back door to play at the park. She breathed a sigh of thanks that Matthew was old enough to be at the park with his sister. The first few times they went alone she asked Jonathan to keep an eye on them, but it was clear Matthew could handle the responsibility.

When the doorbell rang, Carrie opened it to see Kara with an Asian teenager holding a backpack standing beside her. The girl looked terrified.

"Hello! Come on in." They followed her into the house and Carrie went to the table. "Coffee or tea?"

Kara said she'd love a coffee, so while it was brewing Carrie made a hot chocolate for the girl who still hadn't said a word. Bringing the drinks to the table, she sat down with them.

"Carrie, this is Jaz. Jaz, this is my good friend Carrie."

The girl didn't even look at Carrie, gazing off to the side.

"Jaz is about three months pregnant. She just told her parents today and they insisted she leave."

There was the slightest tremble to the girl's chin, and Carrie's heart broke for her. Reaching across the table she gently put her hand on Jaz's arm. "I'm so sorry to hear that. Being pregnant is one of the times when we need support the most. I know you don't know me at all, but I've been through some tough stuff and survived. I'm happy to be here for you, if you'll let me."

Tears began to flow down Jaz's cheeks. "OK" she whispered.

"Would you like to stay here for a little while? I have to warn you, I have a quiet eleven year old son and a very loud, but very cute six year old daughter. She'll probably decide you're her new best friend. You'd have to share a bathroom with the rest of us because this house only has one bathroom, but we could give you a bit of privacy downstairs." Carrie wondered if she had said too much at once. This girl looked like she'd head for the hills at a second's notice.

"Yes please," she whispered.

Carrie looked at Kara. "Is there anything else we should talk about?"

"Jaz is eighteen, so she's legally an adult. She's healthy, but anxiety is a big challenge for her." She turned to Jaz, "I'm sorry. It seems like I'm talking as if you're not here. I think I'm just trying to save you from having to talk. Is that OK? I'm not offended easily so say whatever you want."

"No, please talk."

"Alright. Well, medically speaking the best thing for Jaz right now is to be in a safe place, without stress, where she can work out what she wants to do next. She does have her own bank account that has some money in it so she can buy anything she might need."

"You keep that money for yourself. I want you to have some time here with as little stress as possible. OK?"

Jaz nodded.

Kara stood up, "I have to get going. But I'm happy to leave you two to get to know each other. And Jaz, you have my cell number. Text me whenever OK?"

Again Jaz nodded, and Kara got up to leave. She mouthed 'thank you' to Carrie at the door and then she was jogging down the path to her van. Carrie went back to the table and prayed that she'd say the right thing.

"The kids are playing at the playground around the corner but they'll be back soon. You don't have to talk if you don't want to, but is there anything you want me to know before they come back?"

Jaz finally made eye contact before dropping her gaze again. "I'm sorry."

Carrie waited, but there was nothing more. "Hon, you're not in trouble with me, and you definitely haven't done anything wrong to me… And I hope you'll see one day that this is not the end for you. It might be a different story than you thought you'd have, but different will be ok."

Again the tears fell silently. Carrie grabbed a Kleenex box from the living room and brought it over. The sound of kids in the backyard made her turn to the window with a smile, and when she looked back Jaz had hidden the signs of her sadness.

"Hi Mommy! We're back! Uncle Jonathan was there with Angela and he pushed us both really high on the — *who* are *you*?" She stopped short at the strange person sitting at her table.

Surprisingly, Jaz smiled, "I'm Jaz. Who are you?"

"I'm Katie. And this is Matthew. And this is our house. But you can stay here. That's a funny name."

"It's short for Jasmine. But I prefer Jaz."

Katie's eyes got wide, "Like Princess Jasmine! And you have skin like hers! Are you a princess?"

"Nope, definitely not a princess."

"Well I think you are." Katie announced with finality. "Mommy, we need drinks!"

"Go ahead."

"But Mommy! I'm going to spill again. Pleeeeeease pour for me?"

"If you spill we'll clean it up. Go ahead, you can do this."

They all watched as Katie got out four cups and struggled to carry the jug of lemonade to the counter. With shaking arms she managed to pour four half-full glasses. "I did it!" she shouted triumphantly.

Then she brought the glasses over to everyone sitting at the table. "Lemonade's better than hot chocolate in the summer," she said as she took Jaz's mug away.

"Katie, it would be a better idea if you asked Jaz if she was done with her hot chocolate."

"Are you done?"

"Yeah, thanks." Again Jaz gave Katie a smile, and Carrie could see a hint of the vibrant person that was hiding under all her sadness.

CHAPTER 38

They quickly fell into a new routine with their changing family. Jaz was always quiet, considerate, and helpful. Except for the sound of her retching every morning as she struggled to get past her morning sickness, there was nothing bad about having her there. Each morning she would tidy up her bedding and belongings and insist that the kids still enjoy their playroom during the day.

She was fascinated by Carrie's business and how it was possible to make a living doing something artistic. She was a natural at social media and quickly learned her way around the *Framed* website too. "You have to at least get on Facebook and Instagram," she insisted. Carrie was reluctant to add any more demands but Jaz promised she'd take care of it all. "Since you won't let me pay rent, this will let me help you out."

A few days later she had all of Carrie's friends sharing Framed posts, and again sales started to creep higher. "OK, if you're going to make more business for me then I need help with painting more frames!" Half joking, Carrie was relieved when Jaz agreed. Her only challenge was trying to make things perfect. It turned into an analogy that Carrie would often use, "We're not looking for perfect, here. Just decent. And often decent becomes perfect all on its own."

One week after she arrived, Jaz joined Carrie at the table early in the morning while she was savoring her coffee and making a 'to do' list. They had discovered that tiny sips of tea and some dry toast for Jaz early in the morning seemed to help keep the nausea at bay.

Sitting across from Carrie, she opened up. "I've decided to keep the baby if I can. Do you think I can?"

Surprised, Carrie answered, "Of course you can. It's entirely your choice. Trust me, there are way worse things in life than being a single mom. And I think being a mom is the most amazing thing in the world."

"Not according to my mom. When I told her I was pregnant she said I had destroyed *her* entire life and she'd never forgive me."

"Ouch."

"Yeah. Getting pregnant was definitely not in their plan for me. Actually, it's the first thing I've ever done without their permission. I tried so hard to be the perfect daughter and make them proud. The one time I don't it wrecks everything."

"Do they know the sperm donor?" She smiled at Jaz's shocked face, "I don't think guys should be called fathers unless they earn it by being there. But that's just me."

"They know him, but they don't know he's the...donor. He's actually the son of their best friends. They decided we should study together while they went out to the symphony together. That's when it... happened. It was just one time. I don't even know why I did it. He seemed like he really liked me and I thought he'd like me more. When I told him I was pregnant he begged me not to tell his parents. He promised me he'd help out with money if I never told anyone... You're the first person I've told."

"OK, it's definitely your choice whether anyone else knows or not. I totally respect that."

Jaz smirked, "My mom thinks it's a white boy. She'll sure be surprised when the baby comes out all Asian…Well, if she ever sees the baby."

"Do you think she'll come around?"

"Probably not. I'm an only child, and now I've destroyed the honor of my family. I was supposed to start pre-med this fall. My parents wanted me to become a surgeon."

"What do you want?"

"Me? It's not up to me."

"Actually it is. It's completely up to you. I know culturally your parents expect you to follow their plan. But they're not in your life right now. And even if they were, it's important that you do what's right for you, even if it's not in their plans."

Jaz sighed, "White people are so different from Asians."

"Well, you're stuck with us now. And as my little sister from a different mother I'm officially declaring you part of my family." She came around and put her arm around Jaz and gave her a squeeze before making another coffee. "Hey, thanks again for getting those listings up yesterday. You've got a really artistic eye when it comes to setting them up and photographing them!"

"It's so much fun! I haven't been able to do anything creative for a while because my parents made me quit sewing class so I could add another 'real' course to my schedule."

"You sew?"

"I used to. My grandma was a seamstress. I'd go to her house on the weekends and she'd teach me all sorts of stuff. I think she would've been happy to know she was getting a great-grandchild. At least I hope so. She passed away two years ago." Suddenly Jaz sat back and covered her mouth. "Oh my gosh. I'm talking your ear off. Sorry!"

"Don't be! It's called a conversation, and it's way nicer when *you're* talking too."

Katie joined them downstairs and crawled into Carrie's lap for a morning cuddle. "See?" she said to Jaz, "Best thing in the world."

"Good morning Katie!"

"Good morning Princess Jasmine!"

Jaz rolled her eyes and pretended to be annoyed, but then she smiled. Both kids had completely accepted her as family, and they were able to give her all the hugs and cuddles she needed right now. Carrie couldn't have planned a better set-up for a newly pregnant teenager if she tried. If only Jaz's parents would come around. She knew Jaz frequently checked her phone for messages from them but so far she hadn't heard anything.

"Hey, the kids have been invited to go swimming with friends this afternoon. After I drop them off do you want to come with me while I go thrift store shopping?" Jaz had yet to leave the house, but Carrie didn't want to push too hard.

"Um, yeah. Thanks!"

That afternoon Carrie had the pleasure of introducing Jaz to the magical world of bargain shopping. For a girl that had worn name brand clothes her entire life, Jaz was shocked. Soon she had an armful of clothes. "These are so cool! I can totally change them up to fit me when I start to show." Her face fell, "Oh wait, I forgot I don't have a sewing machine."

"I do, and you can use it anytime. And what a good idea! I have to tell you, my experience with maternity clothes was that they have way too many bows and ribbons."

"Gross. I hate cheesy girly stuff. But with these I think I can be a hip momma."

"Atta girl!"

CHAPTER 39

Carrie found that her own life experiences and the things she was learning in school became woven into almost every conversation she had with Jaz. Things like having boundaries, and knowing it was her right to speak up for what was—or wasn't—good for her. For someone who had spent her entire life trying to do what everyone else thought she should do, it was hard for Jaz to accept.

"But it's selfish to focus on what I want. If we all just did what we wanted there would be chaos, and no respect for anyone else." They were both standing at the table working on painting frames while the kids watched a DVD in the living room.

"Well, yes and no. If we try to get what we want by taking away what is rightfully someone else's then yeah, that would be terrible. *But* if we really listen to what we want deep down inside and we focus on meeting our needs in healthy, respectful ways then the whole world would be a better place."

Jaz bumped her shoulder into Carrie's, "Now who's the Disney Princess with the magical song?"

Laughing, Carrie admitted it did sound too perfect. "But I really think that when we start doing what's best for us we become happier. Too many people go around waiting for someone, or something else to make them happy, when the key is inside of them."

Feeling like she wasn't quite saying things the right way, Carrie spent some time online looking for solutions. It was a luxury to search for things and follow links just for interest's sake, instead of focusing on just what she needed for the next paper, like she had to do for school.

One e-book title caught her eye and she downloaded it to her phone before going to bed. Then she decided she was too curious and brought her phone up with her to start reading it. *Love Yourself Like Your Life Depends on It.* She hated the cover—it looked dark and scary —but was willing to look past it if it was as good as the reviews said.

Less than hour later she set her phone down, feeling a little stunned. *Could it really be that simple?* She knew from her studies that thoughts had incredible power over behaviors and even feelings. But could just saying 'I love myself' over and over change someone's life? There was only one way to find out—with a plan in mind she fell asleep.

"Okey dokey!" Everyone looked up from their breakfast. It was Friday, and they were enjoying a relaxing breakfast together before Carrie and Jaz got started on more frames. "After breakfast we are going to do something new, and maybe a little weird."

Katie said, "Yay!" at the same time as Matthew asked, "Do we have to?"

Smiling, Carrie answered, "Technically this is all in your head so I can't *make* you. But it's a good thing so I really, really hope you do. I read this amazing book last night about loving yourself."

"I love *you* Mommy!"

"Yes, I know you do Katie-girl. But do you love Katie as much as you love Mommy?"

Katie paused, confused. "I don't know."

"See, the thing is we're usually pretty good at loving each other, but maybe not so good at loving ourselves. So sometimes that's why we feel super sad or stressed and we don't know why. It's because we're not loving ourselves."

Wrapping her arms around herself, Katie shook her head, "It's not the same. I want Mommy hugs not Katie hugs."

Out of the corner of her eye, Carrie saw Jaz listening carefully. "You can have all the Mommy hugs you want. And I guess, loving yourself is like a mind hug. All you have to do is find a comfy place, play some nice music, close your eyes, and picture God standing by you and giving you lots of loving sunshine around your body while you say I love myself with every breath."

"And then what happens?"

Carrie was relieved Matthew seemed interested, "Well, we'd set the timer for five minutes to start. I tried it this morning in my room, and after five minutes I felt all relaxed, like after I've been in the hot tub. And I really did feel happier too."

"Cool."

"I want us to try doing it every day. But during the day whenever you want you can say 'I love myself' lots. It will help your brain remember how much you're loved! And—" she looked at Jaz, "—it will make everything in your body feel loved too."

Jaz smiled, "Alright, alright. I'm in." She pulled out her phone and her ever-present ear buds. "I'll do it in the basement."

Since Matthew and Katie didn't have a source of music, Carrie picked a 'sleep' CD she sometimes used, and set it up in the living room. They all got comfy and she set the timer on her phone for five minutes.

Carrie found it a lot harder to concentrate with kids around then when she was alone in her bedroom, but after a minute or two she felt her body relaxing. Breathe in, *I love myself*, breathe out anything else her mind brought up, breathe in, *I love myself*, breathe out…

When her phone started to chime she reluctantly opened her eyes. The kids both looked so peaceful, and Matthew had a little smile. "I liked it," he declared. If only they had known about this earlier.

Jaz came back up and together she and Carrie started to set things up for painting. "Where'd you get that from—the 'I love myself' stuff?" Carrie told her about the e-book and Jaz downloaded it before turning to the frames. Today they were working on two groups of mismatched frames with the classic antique gold finish.

Jaz popped her headphones in and Carrie thought about…her thoughts. She hadn't paid much attention in the past to what she thought about, but it seemed like it wasn't all good. Things like worrying about money could completely take over her thoughts at any time. And now that Don was probably out of jail she worried about whether he'd try to see the kids. Sometimes she thought about Jonathan—which always made her smile until she started worrying about whether it could work between them or not.

She decided to try and focus on the whole 'I love myself' thing and try to worry less. It was definitely easier to stop worrying when she had something else to say to herself.

By lunchtime Carrie decided they had done enough for the week. She'd pack up the two orders that were booked to go out tomorrow morning, and that was it. It took a few tries to get Jaz to quit too. She always wanted to make sure she did enough to make Carrie happy. But finally she admitted she was keen to do some sewing. They moved the frames to the basement to keep drying and set up the sewing machine at the table in the basement.

Carrie would have loved to just sit and watch Jaz, but the kids were getting squirrely. They decided to go to one of the nature reserves in the area to explore, and collect any cans and bottles laying around. Having time to do whatever they wanted was nice, and Carrie knew Jaz would enjoy some peace and quiet while they were gone.

CHAPTER 40

August was hot, sunny, and brought some unwelcome news. First, Carrie's old neighbor Mr. Morris called.

"Mr. Morris! What a nice surprise. Goodness, I haven't talked to you in so long—"

"—I'm afraid I have some bad news for you Carrie. I just got a call from my tenant. At the house you used to live in. Don was there, looking for you. The poor lady was terrified. She said at first he seemed really nice, but then he saw something behind her that he thought was yours, and he started yelling."

"Oh my gosh. The poor lady! I guess that means he's out of jail..."

"Well, at least she told me, but she's pretty shaken up. I told her to report it to the police, and she said she would. But you need to be careful Carrie."

"I will, well, I'll try. Thanks for letting me know, and I'm so sorry Don's crap is still following you."

"Don't worry about me my dear. You just take care of yourself and the kids. How are you doing?"

Carrie told him about the kids, their new home, her business, and school. He was impressed, and asked for her website twice so he could look at it. After she hung up she had to fight the same anxiety she used to feel whenever she knew she had to face Don. *I love myself, I love myself* she told herself while she tried to slow her breathing.

The kids came in the back door, laughing after being at the playground for the last forty-five minutes. Matthew went to the freezer to get popsicles for each of them. "It's so hot out there! Can we go to the pool this afternoon?"

"Yeah, sure," Carrie absent-mindedly replied. *Should she warn the kids? Could Don even find them? What about Jaz?* Jaz had started going out on her own and was becoming more confident in making choices for herself. Carrie didn't want anything to stand in the way of her progress.

Before she could answer her own questions, she got a text from Lauren:

> *that girl who moved to the townhouse after us just texted me. some freaky dude was there looking for you. she said he was pissed off*

Carrie looked up at the sky. *Seriously? How many innocent people was Don going to scare before he got what he wanted?* Trying to think clearly, she texted back:

> *Second place he's been to today then. I guess he's out of jail. Can you ask her to report it? I know he didn't do anything, but at least they'll know he's out there and angry. I don't think he can find me though. I hope not.*

A few minutes later Lauren replied:

> *she called the police but they might be a while cuz he already left. do u want us to come stay with u*

Tears stung Carrie's eyes. She was so lucky to have such good friends!

> *No, but thank you so much. I'm going to take the kids swimming and then I'll try to figure out what to do. I've got money for a lawyer if I need, thanks to all your help with the business.*

Lauren sent back a stream of heart emojis.

"All right kids. Let's go swimming! Um, just pack swimsuits and towels. We'll change there." She sent a text to Jaz saying they'd be at the pool for a few hours and then went to get her own swimming stuff.

Just as they were about to get their shoes on, Carrie glanced out the front window and felt terror completely absorb her body. A man looking exactly like Don slowly drove past, looking at the houses. She breathed out when he passed. It couldn't be him. There's no way he could know she was here. But she needed to calm down before they left the house.

"Hey, um, guys. I think I should use the bathroom before we go. Do you each want to grab a cookie while you wait?"

"YAY!" Katie shouted and ran to the kitchen.

Matthew turned to follow her and stopped suddenly. "Mom" he whispered, staring out the window. Carrie followed his gaze. Don was getting out of an older model black car.

"Quick! Into the laundry room!" Carrie ran to the kitchen and grabbed Katie, Matthew was right behind her.

"SHHHH!" she told Katie firmly, trying to get some control over her pounding heart. The sound of a hand slamming against the front door made them all jump.

"CARRIE!" he roared, "YOU CAN'T HIDE FROM ME! GET YOUR LAME ASS OUT HERE!"

"Mommy!" Katie whimpered. Carrie was crouching on the floor in front of the washer, with Katie curled in a ball in her lap. She had one arm around Katie, and one around Matthew who was also crouching, his entire body vibrating with fear.

Think! Think! Carrie told herself. The nightmares were all coming back to her in an onslaught of darkness and screaming. She had to get the kids away from him. Now.

"OK, listen to me" she whispered. "I need you two to very quietly go out the back and run to Uncle Johnny's, OK? You'll be safe there. Stay with him until I come get you, no matter what."

"But Mom, I don't have my shoes on…" Matthew whispered back. The pounding started again.

"You just have to go, OK? Keep your sister with you. Make sure she stays with you, and be quiet until you're there. I'm going to take care of this."

Matthew looked up at her. There were tears in his eyes. "OK Mom. I love you."

"I love you too." She hugged them both and then carefully opened the back door. "Run!"

In seconds they were across the yard and out the gate into the back alley. She closed the door and pulled out her phone, but before she could dial she heard Don's voice again.

"TELL ME WHERE CARRIE IS YOU LITTLE CHINK!"

Without thinking, Carrie ran to the front door and threw it open. Jaz was standing on the sidewalk behind Don. Her shaking hands were up as if to defend herself.

"Leave her alone Don!"

"Well, well, well. If it isn't my pathetic wife. WHERE ARE MY KIDS CARRIE?"

"They're not here. You need to leave Don. This is completely unacceptable." Carrie let her body lean against the door frame, hoping he wouldn't see her shaking. She didn't care what he might try to do now, as long as he left Jaz alone.

"I'M NOT GOING UNTIL I HAVE THE KIDS. YOU CAN'T HIDE THEM FROM ME! I HAVE A LEGAL RIGHT TO BE HERE, AND YOU'RE GOING TO BE REAL SORRY FOR BEING SUCH A BITCH!"

Carrie saw Jaz slowly reach down and grab her phone. She caught her eye and nodded slightly. Right now, she was so glad for all the talks they had had about boundaries. Quietly Jaz backed up a few steps and held the phone up to talk.

"You are yelling and threatening me. I'm asking you to leave. Now."

Instead, Don took a step towards Carrie. His eyes were bulging and his nose was flaring with each gasp of breath. In the back of her mind, Carrie flashed back to when her dad was helping her move out. He had told Don in no uncertain terms that the way he was treating Carrie was wrong. Don had shot back in defense, "I've never hit her!" If he did hit her now, Jaz was watching. But she knew words were Don's favorite weapon.

"YOU'VE KEPT THOSE KIDS AWAY FROM ME ON PURPOSE AND I HAVE EVERY RIGHT TO TAKE THEM NOW!"

Out of the corner of her eye, Carrie saw Jonathan run up and stop beside Jaz. He was in his bare feet, but looked ready to take on anyone. She gave him just a short shake of her head and turned back to Don. It was time to face her ex-husband.

"Don, this is MY space, and you have no right to be in it. I asked you to leave and I meant it. You've already had at least two harassment complaints filed against you today by the people you've tried to use to get to me. I'll be the next one to file. I'm quite sure the terms of your release require some level of decent behavior. Now take yourself OFF my porch NOW!"

He took a breath in and raised his finger towards Carrie.

"The police are on their way Carrie!" Despite her fear, Jaz managed to make her voice ring loud and clear.

Don spun around to her, and stopped at the small, pregnant teenager with a phone in her hand, and the tall man standing behind her, his arms crossed and his glare unwavering. Carrie could see Don struggling to control himself now that he saw Carrie wasn't alone.

"The neighbors have a couple of security cameras Don. I think it's time I got some too. Everything you do now might be used against you."

He stormed past Jaz and Jonathan and got into the car. For a second Carrie felt frozen, and then her brain kicked in. She ran after him, and was just in time to catch the license plate on the car as the tires squealed away. Grabbing her phone, she typed it in, and then held it up for Jaz to see.

Jaz gave the dispatcher the license plate number, and then handed the phone to Carrie. "Hello? Yes, sir. I'm Carrie. His name is Don Bennet, and he just got out of jail for drunk driving. I'm pretty sure his license is suspended...he's in a black car...headed, um, west I think on 95th Ave...The kids are at a friend's. Yes, they're safe there... OK, thank you."

She handed the phone back to Jaz, who hung up. "Are you OK?" she put her arms around the girl and Jaz collapsed into her. As she held her she looked at Jonathan, and she knew that he would do anything to protect her, if she needed. But somehow he had understood that she had to stand up to Don herself this time. He had been there for her, giving her the courage to face her demon.

"Come on, let's get you sitting down. That was quite a terrible thing to see." She hoped the incident hadn't harmed the baby in any way.

Back inside, Jonathan assured her that the kids were safe with Chris, and would stay there for as long as needed. He sent Chris a quick text to update him and then turned back to Carrie. All she wanted was to curl up in his arms and forget about anything, but she needed to focus on Jaz.

"The police should be here soon," Jaz's voice was shaky again. Carrie wrapped her arm around her and tried to breathe slowly. Her own heart was still pounding. On the other side of her she felt Jonathan take her hand and envelop it in his. Almost instantly she started to calm down.

It took almost half an hour to give the police their statements after they arrived. Carrie was grateful for the woman who sat with Jaz and questioned her so gently. She and Jonathan also told their versions, and she gave them Mr. Morris and Lauren's contact information so they could corroborate the different events.

After the police left, Jaz assured her that she would be OK on her own while Jonathan and Carrie went to get the kids. Carrie grabbed Matthew's shoes, and hand in hand they jogged back to Jonathan's to get the kids.

CHAPTER 41

They never went swimming that day. Instead, Jonathan ordered Chinese take-out and they ate together at home. Carrie didn't want to push anyone to talk about it, but the conversation seemed to flow there.

"Mommy, did jail make Daddy a bad person?"

"No Katie. Your daddy chose to try and control people around him instead of facing the things inside of him that are making him angry. And he made those choices long before he went to jail."

"Like when he made us leave his house in our pajamas and said he never wanted to see us again?"

Carrie flinched at the memory, "Yeah. Instead of facing his own problem with not paying the rent, he tried to make you and Matthew upset."

"And you Mommy. He made you cry. I don't like that."

There was quiet for a few minutes before Jaz spoke up, "For Chinese food this isn't bad."

Everyone laughed, lightening the mood a bit. "I lived in Singapore for a few years, and I've been working my way through every Asian restaurant here," said Jonathan. "So far this is the winner. I'm glad you sort of like it."

Jaz smiled, then looked at Carrie, "I didn't know your ex was like that. I thought all the advice you were giving me was because you learned it in school. But...I guess today I realized you're strong because you choose to be. It's not just words to you. It's cool."

"I wish he went back to jail," Matthew said. His voice was tight and he held his back stiff.

Jonathan reached over and put a hand on his shoulder, "No matter what happens next, you can count on your mom looking out for you, and I'll always be close by if you need."

He relaxed just a fraction, "I was really glad you ran back to be with Mom. I wanted to go help her too but I didn't want to leave Katie."

"You all made me so proud today. It was a nasty situation that none of us deserved. But everyone stayed calm and safe. Really, you are the best." Carrie looked around the table. It was good to have five at the table. She felt supported and loved by everyone there.

The trauma of that day left a lasting impression on all of them, but the *I love myself* times really helped. Carrie thought that the nightmares would return in full force, but they didn't. It was as if facing one of her biggest fears gave her brain the chance it needed to move on.

The next morning Jaz was already up when Carrie came down. "Couldn't sleep?"

"No, but nothing bad. I had some ideas about those clothes I was working on. Can I bring them up and show you?"

"Yeah, of course."

When Jaz came up the stairs Carrie nearly dropped her cup. She looked pregnant sure, but amazing. A boho tunic had been altered to fit her shoulders and upper body perfectly, and although it looked fitted, there were some gathers at the front that would easily grow with the baby.

And the ripped jean shorts she was wearing underneath... "You can't actually do up those shorts, can you?"

Jaz lifted up her top to show the panel she had sewn into the top of the shorts to give space. Again, the way she had made the shorts fit looked so comfortable. "Seriously? Wow! How did you know to do this?"

"It's all stuff my grandma did all the time—altering clothes. And the stuff at the thrift store is so cool! Here, hang on..."

She brought up some t-shirts that would clearly fit a pregnant woman. "I had to put a pillow under the shirt to figure out what size to make them."

"I don't remember seeing any of these shirts there, and I looked through the women's clothes."

"These were men's shirts. I wanted extra fabric to work with." She held up what looked like a denim jacket, "What do you think of this?"

"Um, can you put it on?...Holy cow Jaz, you're a genius!" It was a classic denim jacket, except in the front it was cut out at a curve on each side from the bust down to the side seams. Perfect fit, a cool look, and room for a belly. Jaz lifted her arms and spun around. From the back it looked like a regular denim jacket, but from the front it looked like nothing Carrie had ever seen before.

"I thought I could add in a black fleece insert that's removable, but could zip in here," she pointed to where she had cut out the jacket, "and then zip it up like a regular hoodie over my stomach when it's bigger."

"Have you always been able to do this with clothes?"

"I never designed my own stuff, but I'm ok at sewing...I wish I would have taken a clothing design course at school. This was so much fun. I kinda forgot about all the bad stuff for a while."

Carrie smiled, "Jaz, I think you're on to something here."

"There's just one thing…I need your help."

"Of course! What is it? Wait, are you blushing?"

Jaz groaned and hid her face. "I need bigger bras," she mumbled from behind her hands.

"Well, they do say there's a first time for everything, even a something like needing more…support." Carrie was tempted to giggle, although she felt for Jaz who was so private about things like that.

"I don't even know where to go. My mom always bought them for me."

"Oh, I see. No problem. Hey, how about I see if Jonathan can take the kids for a bit tomorrow and you and I go to the mall together? You can wear your cool clothes and we'll go laugh at the cheesy preggo clothes before we get you some new underwear. You're going to need everything eventually."

"Cool! Thanks!"

Jonathan suggested he take the kids mini golfing and then they could all meet up for a late lunch. Knowing that he'd be nearby made Carrie feel better about going out. The police hadn't been able to locate Don yesterday, but they did confirm that he was banned from driving for five years. In the back of her mind she kept trying to figure out how he had found her so quickly.

The air conditioning was running full blast in the mall, and Jaz and Carrie were both glad they brought jackets along. "Seriously Jaz, the way you re-did that jacket is so cool. It's a lot like what Lauren does with her paintings. You know, repurposing things and making them way better than they were to start."

"Thanks! It took a while to figure out how to finish it after I cut out the center," she smiled shyly, "but I like it too!"

Sure enough, the maternity store didn't really offer much for pregnant women like Jaz. But just as they were getting ready to leave, a customer stopped them. Her perfectly styled blonde hair, full make-up, and brand name clothes screamed *image*. "I love your jacket! Where did you get it?"

"Oh, thank you. I made it."

"No way. It's the coolest maternity jacket I've ever seen."

Carrie couldn't help but step in, "She repurposed it from a vintage jacket. And it has a removable fleece panel that can zip up over the belly for cool weather!"

"Are you kidding?" Waving over another highly made-up woman she turned Jaz to face her, "*Look* at this jacket! It's totally vintage. Don't you love it?"

Carrie felt herself flashing back to her own realization two years ago that people would pay money—a lot of money—for something 'repurposed' or 'vintage'. "You know, she might be branching out into one of a kind maternity clothes. Jaz, why don't you give them your Instagram handle. You'll be putting things up there, right?"

Jaz looked at her, confused. "Um, yeah. OK." Both ladies immediately added her.

"Will you have anything this week? I'm getting *so* tired of *this*," with a dismissive wave, the other lady covered the entire maternity store.

"Yeah, maybe."

Carrie steered Jaz out of the store until they were far enough away to not be overheard. "What do you think Jaz? Feel like becoming a clothing designer?"

"I don't know. Do you really think they liked it?" She fingered the collar of her jacket self-consciously.

"Oh yeah. And with a few women like that wearing your stuff and sharing it on social media you could really go places!" Carrie tried to reel in her enthusiasm. She didn't want to push Jaz. "But it's up to you hon. At least you know that you are going to be the most stylin' momma-to-be in town! Now come on, I think there's a department store where we can get maternity underwear."

Later on, over lunch with the kids and Jonathan, Carrie told the story of how strangers were coming up to Jaz in the mall to compliment her on her jacket. "They even wanted to buy it!"

"Not that I'm an expert or anything," Jonathan looked at Jaz, "but I remember that Jenny ended up ordering maternity clothes online because she couldn't find anything she liked in the stores. It was the only time she blew their budget and Max still teases her about it."

"You know, lots of people use Instagram for shopping now..." Jaz stopped eating and looked out the window.

Carrie hadn't pushed Jaz to find a way to support herself as a single mom. She had been more concerned about showing her love and support than anything else. Although they *had* agreed on a small weekly salary for all the help Jaz was giving with the business. And really, it wasn't practical for Jaz to live with them long term. She was going to need a real room with walls and a door for privacy when the baby arrived.

CHAPTER 42

Over the next few days Jaz was quieter than usual. Carrie tried to give her space, but finally she felt she needed to give her a little nudge. "Have you looked at what you need to earn to support you and your baby?"

Jaz looked surprised, "No!"

"OK, well why don't you start to write down the things you'll need. And if you want I can show you my budget."

Just then Lauren came in with more paintings for sale. After they enjoyed looking through them, they sat at the table. "Cool outfit! Gee, way back when I was pregnant they sure didn't have clothes like this!"

"Ha ha." Jaz replied, "How's Brittany?"

"Driving me crazy! She can only walk a few steps, but between that and grabbing furniture to help get her around she's getting into *everything*. And she gets super mad when we take stuff away!"

"How much does her stuff cost? I mean, how much do you need to have for a baby?"

"Well, at first we hardly had money for anything and it was super hard. I'd keep her in a diaper as long as possible before changing her, and we were all sleeping on the floor. Then Carrie gave me the job doing frames, and Kara gave us all her baby stuff. Things got better after that. I guess you can survive with just a bit of money. But it sucks big time. I'd never have another baby if I didn't have money now." She looked up at Jaz, "Oh, sorry. I didn't mean you. I mean…shit."

"No, it's OK. I just never thought about it. Like, what I should do next…I've never even had a real job. My parent's said it would impact my grades so I wasn't allowed to."

"I worked at McDonald's until I got pregnant. But now, getting paid to paint—it rocks. And I don't have to leave Brittany to go to work. That's really the best part…well that and the crap load of money coming in!"

Carrie was looking at her calendar and broke in, "Hey Lauren, are there any days that won't work for you to come over for an end-of-summer barbeque? I want to have everyone over one more time before I start school again."

"Aw, do you have to go back to school?"

"Why? What's wrong with school?" Jaz wanted to know.

"Because," Lauren interrupted Carrie, "Studying and writing papers becomes her whole life. I'm pretty sure she stops sleeping because she gets pretty grumpy too."

"Hey!" Carrie protested, "It's not that bad!"

Lauren raised her eyebrows.

"OK, OK, I may get a little focused. But I only have to do it for eight more months. And with all the stock we have right now, plus the work my mom keeps doing I won't have to spend so much time working." She looked at Jaz, "If you and I can get the rest of the frames downstairs done in the next week or so, I think I'll be set for the fall. You have been *such* a huge help!"

"Hello!" chimed in Lauren.

Carrie laughed, "Yeah, yeah, you too. Everybody knows your stuff is the star of the business! But I'm really truly grateful for all you've done too."

Jaz was unusually quiet for the rest of the night, even when Katie begged her to play 'babies'. She had used scrap fabric to make Katie some adorable clothes for her dolls, and together they would dress them up in all sorts of outfits.

"I wish I had clothes like this," Katie sighed dramatically.

Carrie called out from the kitchen where she was making a coffee, "Hey! You've got more clothes than ever before Katie-girl. And we'll get you some fun clothes when we go back to school shopping in a few days."

"I know, but these clothes are *special.* Not like the boring ones at the store."

"What about you Matthew?" Jaz interrupted.

"Huh?" he was so engrossed in his video game he had been ignoring the conversation around him.

"Do you like your clothes?"

"Well..." he looked at Carrie as she walked into the room with her favorite mug.

"I already know, bud. It's OK to say it out loud."

"Sorry Mom, but I don't really like the clothes you buy me. Some stuff is OK. Like that dress shirt I wore for Christmas not last year but the year before."

Jaz got out her phone and went to sit beside him. After a few seconds of typing, she showed him her screen. "What about this stuff?"

"Cool! Yeah, I like that. And this one with the bow tie? I mean, I wouldn't wear it to school. But I like it. There's no clothes like this where we shop."

Carrie ended up delaying the back-to-school shopping so she could have everyone over for dinner before Kara, Ken and their boys left for a week of camping. Jonathan offered to take her to Costco, and they came back with enough food to feed everyone twice over, plus almost half of the school supplies she needed for the kids. It was fun having his help to get ready, and more than a few times Carrie found herself watching him when she should have been getting together burger toppings.

Granted, he managed to make an epic mess in the kitchen, but he was trying. And when everything was done he sat on the couch and played Nintendo Switch with Matthew until people started coming. Then Carrie sent the rowdiest kids to the basement and the younger kids outside while the adults visited.

It was Jaz's first introduction to Carrie's wider circle of friends, and Carrie was proud to introduce her to everyone. Although Jaz was quiet, she was trying hard to make conversation. When Carrie's old landlord Mr. Morris arrived (a last-minute inspiration since she hadn't seen him in over a year), Jaz sat and visited with him until it was time to eat.

Later on, she saw Lisa visiting with Jaz. Although Lisa had a wonderful relationship with her mom now, she had left home at eighteen without any support from her parents. Lisa and Jaz probably had a lot in common.

CHAPTER 43

Carrie tried not to groan as she looked at her list. She really should have gotten the back-to-school shopping done by now. As it stood, she'd be fighting the crowds to get the last of the supplies, and there were new clothes that the kids needed too. She suspected a part of her was really dreading going back to grad school and so she had been avoiding everything to do with it.

"What's wrong?" As usual, Jaz was completely silent when she walked up the stairs, and Carrie hadn't heard her coming.

"Oh, just dreading shopping. I mean, it's OK. It's not like before when we had to register with a charity to get supplies and the kids were stuck with whatever clothes they already had. I shouldn't complain I guess. I just don't want to do it."

Jaz smiled, "Oh good, I have something for you then. But I also have something to tell you…"

"Take your time! I'd much rather sit here with you than go get stuff done." Carrie took another sip of her coffee and waited.

"I'm really, really glad you let me stay here. It's been…uh…you *are* like a big sister. I've always wanted that. And I love your kids."

"They love you too!"

"I know, and I want to still see them lots. But I've decided to move out."

Carrie bit back a complaint. This is what she had been focusing on — getting Jaz to take control of her life. But she really didn't want her to leave! "Tell me more!"

"Well the other night at your party? I was talking to Lisa. And she's got this room in her house that's free because her friend just got married and moved out."

They had all been thrilled for Amy who recently married Lisa's old neighbor Jesse. They now lived about an hour away in the town Lisa grew up in.

"You're going to live with Lisa?" Jazz nodded, "Oh Jaz, that's wonderful! I don't want you to move out, but if you have to go anywhere else, I'd choose Lisa's."

"Yeah, she's pretty nice. And she's got an extra room that I can use to do my sewing and she said I only need to pay rent for it if I start to make money on my designs."

"Wow! So you're moving out *and* starting your business?"

"Uh huh! I've had a ton of followers since I started putting up those pics of my maternity outfits. You were right, everyone's crazy to get clothes that are actually cool. And…there's something else. But I need to wait until your kids are up."

Matthew came slowly down the stairs just then. Carrie smiled, "He'll be 'up' in about half an hour." She was intrigued at what Jaz might need the kids for. Whatever it was, they'd be happy to help her, she was sure of that.

After breakfast, everyone was awake enough for whatever Jaz had up her sleeve. "OK, so Carrie, you need to go sit on the couch and wait for us. Katie and Matthew, come with me."

There was a lot of chatter coming from the basement, but Carrie couldn't make out what they were saying.

"Don't look Mommy!" Katie giggled as she ran upstairs to her room with her arms full. Matthew and Jaz followed her, also carrying things, and after a few minutes Jaz came down alone.

"Are you ready for the world's most stylish kids? Because here they come!"

Matthew came downstairs first, wearing a pair of dark blue jeans that were tight around the ankles, a white dress shirt that had a contrasting band of blue paisley fabric along the pocket, under the collar, and behind the buttons, and a bright blue bow tie. He was so proud he was almost strutting, and he couldn't keep the huge smile off his face. Carrie was literally speechless.

"Pretty cool, huh mom? It's even better than the pictures I saw on Jaz's phone!"

"Me next!" Katie called from the top of the stairs. She was wearing a short, sparkly pink dress with a rainbow of ribbons sewn on it that ran from her shoulder to her waist. The dress was gathered at the waist before falling in a soft ruffle just above Katie's knees. Instead of tights (which Katie always complained about wearing) she was wearing knee high white socks that had a little rainbow with the same ribbons on each side. She skipped down the stairs before giving a big twirl and then running to hug Jaz. "I'm so BEAUTIFUL!"

"Jaz, I'm amazed! It's like you somehow managed to put the kids' personalities into their clothes! They couldn't be dressed more perfectly!"

"Well, they still need shoes. I couldn't do that without your help. And I have a few cool t-shirts for Matthew for school, plus some skirts and tops for Katie. I just wanted you to see these ones first."

"I don't know how I can ever thank you for this!"

"Can I use them as models? For my Instagram page. These clothes are theirs to keep. But when I do more, I'd like them to model the clothes. I'm going to charge a lot for them. My mom would pay almost anything to have me wearing the 'right' things for school, so I just need to find other moms like her."

"Where did you get the fabric?"

Jaz smiled proudly, "You really have to ask?"

"NO! You did not! I'm in those stores every week! There's no way this stuff was all there!"

"Well, not *exactly* these clothes. But the original stuff all came from thrift stores. Matthew's jeans were the right size, I just changed them to be like skinny jeans but more comfortable. And Katie's dress was a curtain, so that was pretty easy. Oh, her socks I bought new and just added the rainbows."

"If you tell me what else they need for school clothes I can get it done before they start school. And before I move." Jaz looked mournfully at the kids.

Tears filled Katie's eyes, "You're moving?"

She crouched down a bit awkwardly beside Katie. Her belly was definitely starting to change how she moved, "I am. It's time for you to have your mommy to yourself again. And I need to get ready to have my own baby."

"But I wanted you to have your baby HERE!"

"I promise I'll bring him over every week to visit, OK?"

Katie sniffed and nodded, "OK, but it's a her not a him."

Ignoring the last comment, Jaz stood up and faced Carrie, "Could I come with you to pick out shoes? I have a look in mind. And then I want to use the pictures of the kids in these outfits for my page."

"Jaz, you're doing it." Carrie felt tears in the corners of her own eyes, but unlike Katie, her tears were a mixture of pride and happiness, "You're making your own path. I'm so proud of you, and so happy we know you." She laughed through her tears, "And I'm *so* grateful you saved me from shopping for clothes!"

"I'm going to make some stuff for you too. I just wanted to get the kids' done before you went shopping."

"That is really good news." She got up and hugged Jaz before giving an exaggerated bow, "I hereby dub thee the master of my image!"

Katie giggled. "You're silly."

Matthew asked if he could go show Jonathan his new outfit. Carrie agreed but warned him to be careful with his new clothes. She wouldn't let Katie out of the house in her outfit until Jaz had the photos she wanted.

CHAPTER 44

"So, big week for you." Jonathan smiled at Carrie from across the table and she felt her breath catch. It had been a long time since they had been alone together. Jaz had insisted on babysitting the kids so they could go on a real date—Jaz's words.

With help from Jaz, she was also enjoying some new clothes. Tonight she had on an ocean green wrap dress with a deep neckline accented by a hint of silver, and the same silver around the hem. Jaz had made an ordinary (and very comfortable) dress into something that set off Carrie's complexion and made her feel special and beautiful. The look was finished with silver bracelets, silver dangly earrings, and Jaz had insisted Carrie put her hair up in a messy bun with wisps of curls hanging down.

The first thing Jonathan did when she opened the door was step back and drop his jaw. "Uh...wow!"

"Isn't Mommy beautiful?" Katie piped up from the kitchen table where she was coloring with Jaz.

Jonathan cleared his throat. "Is there a word for more than beautiful?"

"Yep! It's beautifuller!"

"Then your mom is beautifuller!"

Carrie waved goodbye and stepped out. "You're looking good too!" He was wearing a steel grey dress shirt with a white tie that had specks of color through it. His dark dress pants fit him perfectly and his dress shoes were a subtle multicolor pattern that looked incredibly stylish. Carrie looked down at the white strappy sandals Jaz had insisted she buy. Tonight she could almost keep up with him in the style category.

Jonathan drove to an area of the city Carrie wasn't familiar with and parked in front of a place that could have been mistaken for a charming little house. The sign above the door said it offered fine Italian dining and once they were inside Carrie felt herself relaxing as she took in the warmth from the candlelit tables and the gentle sounds of a violin playing.

"Uh, Carrie?" Jonathan brought Carrie back to the present and she smiled at him across the table. He had asked her if she was OK with Jaz moving out.

"Yeah. I'm really pleased that Jaz is finding her feet, but I'm really going to miss her. The house will feel so empty without her!"

"Does that mean you might have room for someone else to be over more often?" He paused as the waitress brought glasses of red wine for each of them. "I mean me, if that wasn't clear."

"Of course, we always have room for you!" She looked at his hand on the table, so close to hers.

"I want more than that. Carrie, I care about you and the kids more than I ever imagined was possible. Can we give us a go? As a couple?" He reached and wrapped his hand around hers. Carrie felt tingles all the way down to her toes.

All of her protests, her reasons for not getting in another relationship, and her insecurities suddenly seemed so very small. Taking a breath and smiling, she answered, "Yeah."

"Seriously? You really mean it?"

"I do. I thought I'd never date again. But you've been changing my mind about that for a while now." She shifted her hand so their fingers were intertwined.

Jonathan picked up his glass, "To the next step, together."

Carrie clinked her glass to his, "To being together."

Hours later, they stood up to leave. Carrie found herself smiling again when Jonathan put his arm around her waist. If this kept up she'd need a muscle relaxant for her face.

At her front door, she turned to look up at him. "I seem to have my face stuck with this smile. I guess I've got you to thank for that."

He smiled back tenderly. Reaching up he caressed her cheek before leaning in and giving her a slow kiss. Carrie stood on her tiptoes and wrapped her hands over his shoulders. It was a kiss to end all kisses, and promised a beautiful beginning.

CHAPTER 45

People spilled out the back doors of Jonathan's house into the newly landscaped backyard. Everywhere there were bright orange streamers and balloons—a fun nod to Carrie's now infamous orange couch. The party to celebrate Carrie's graduation was in full swing.

Jonathan didn't have to look far to see Carrie. She was sitting beside her mom on the porch. At the moment she was in the middle of saying something funny and he could hear her laugh carrying through the noise around him. Her dark hair was pulled back in a high ponytail but there were wisps escaping to blow around her face in the breeze.

Her white summer dress was accented with an orange chunky necklace and a blue belt, and she was wearing the same silver bracelets and white sandals that she had worn the night they had started dating. Catching him staring at her, Carrie smiled, said something to her mom, and walked over to him.

She wrapped an arm around his waist and reached up to kiss his cheek. "It looks like your party planning career is off to a great start!"

He groaned. He had tried so hard to plan it all himself, but with Carrie so busy with school he had begged massive help from all their friends. Jenny claimed she was going to charge him for all the time it took to answer his hourly calls and texts.

"Thanks so much for booking the hotel for my parents. My mom says it has the most beautiful bathroom she's ever seen."

"You're welcome. Although it's Maria who should take the credit. Well, her and Jaz. Apparently they checked out six hotels for accessibility and this was the best one."

Carrie had seen Maria arrive early with Lisa, Jaz, and baby Alexander. Maria used a wheelchair almost all the time now, but Jonathan and Chris had made sure the house would be easily accessible for her and Carrie's mom.

"Those two make quite a pair!" Carrie agreed. Maria had instantly adopted Jaz when she walked in the door, and now she insisted on treating Alexander as a grandson. Jaz had tried to reach out to her parents multiple times, with no success yet. Lisa confided in Carrie that Jaz would often walk Alexander past her parent's house in the hopes that they'd change their mind.

But in the meantime, she and her baby were loved unconditionally by Lisa, Maria, Chris, Carla, and especially Becky who would sit for hours holding toys for him and then watching him sleep.

"Did Chris and Carla get that house?" Carrie knew they had been trying to buy a house, but she had missed news from everyone in the past few weeks as she pushed to finish school on time.

"Yeah, I think they take possession next week, but it's going to be a while before it's livable. I have to say, that guy is quite the visionary. All I saw was a teardown, but he's convinced they can turn it into their dream home." A commotion at the door distracted Jonathan.

Coming in were Jenny's parents! "Grandma!" Angela ran over and clung to her grandma.

Together with Jonathan, Carrie walked over, "Tom, Martha! Hi! I didn't know you were coming!"

Tom winked at Jonathan before turning to Carrie, "Of course! We couldn't miss a chance to celebrate your—" he turned to Jonathan, "—uh, your graduation."

"Well come on over and meet my parents." Carrie turned, and missed the pointed glances that passed between Jonathan and the couple who had become his parents when his brother married Jenny.

Carrie was so busy catching up with everyone that she barely ate. It had been over a month since she had last seen Alexander and she couldn't get over how much he had changed. In her absence, Lauren had taken Jaz under wing and helped her navigate the first few months of motherhood. Brittany was quite possessive of him, and told Carrie "My Ander!" when she sat down with him.

"Of course honey, he's your Alexander." Satisfied that Carrie knew who she was holding, Brittany toddled off to find Matthew—her next favorite person besides her parents. Dustin and Lauren were doing a great job with her. He still was only able to say a few words but a stern look from Daddy was all that was needed for Brittany to behave. Although Lauren often complained to Carrie that she refused to listen at all when he wasn't there to keep her in line!

The only ones missing from the party were Ken, Justin, and Calvin who were away at a rugby tournament for the weekend. While it was good for the older boys to keep busy, Kara was finding it challenging to manage such a busy schedule. Next week Magnus would be back to coming to Carrie's after school two days a week so Ken could coach the older boy's after-school practices. They joked that he had traded in a full-time job for full-time parenting plus full-time coaching.

Carrie was just heading over to sit with her parents when someone started banging their cutlery against a glass. "Speech speech!" She turned to look where the voice was coming from. Jonathan was standing in front of a beautiful rose arbor that was just beginning to blossom. It was her favorite place in his backyard. He waved her over.

She stood beside him and smiled at all of her friends and family. While she'd probably sleep for a few days when the night was over, right now she felt happier than ever before and she wished the moment could be frozen to savor for years to come. Turning to Jonathan she whispered, 'Thank you'.

Everyone got quiet, and Carrie tried to think about how to thank them all. "I don't really know where to start. But all of you have become such an important part of my life."

From her grandpa's lap Katie piped up, "Me too!"

Everyone laughed and Carrie continued, "Yep, my life and my kid's lives. I truly feel so blessed tonight. Thank you all so much." She turned to look at Jonathan, who was looking decidedly nervous, "And thank you Jonathan for going to so much work to celebrate today."

Instead of smiling back, he released his hand from around her waist and stepped back. Max ran over and slipped something in his hand, and Carrie noticed that people were starting to hold their phones up. But it wasn't until Jonathan kneeled in front of her that she realized what was happening.

"Carrie, when I moved back here I really thought my heart could never love again. But from the very first time I saw you I loved you like I've never loved before. Your heart of pure gold, your sweet soul that always wants to care for the people around you, the way you're a mother to your kids, and a daughter to your parents, and a friend to everyone, it's all part of what makes you the most breathtaking woman in the world. I can't bear to be one block away from you anymore, it's just too far. Carrie Joy Bennet, will you do me the honor of agreeing to marry me."

With tears streaming down her face Carrie couldn't speak, but she could smile and nod. Everyone burst out cheering while Jonathan slipped a ring on her finger and then stood up to give her a long, passionate, stomach tingling kiss. When they finally came up for air, Matthew and Katie were there waiting to hug them.

"Well," Jonathan asked Matthew, "How did I do?"

Matthew smirked. "Not bad."

"What? Matthew, you *knew* about this?"

"Yeah Mom, I had to have a talk with Jonathan about stuff, you know. Because I'm the first guy in your life and everything."

Carrie hugged him fiercely, "You're definitely the first guy in my life, and I love you so much." Looking over her shoulder, Carrie saw her mom crying and gesturing for her to come over. "Grandma wants me, hang on." She went over and was greeted with the sound of her sister squealing through the phone.

"Mom let me watch the whole thing! I'm so excited for you Carrie! Jonathan tried everything to get me to come tonight but I just couldn't get the time off work. But I'll be there for your wedding, even if I have to quit my job."

With tears falling again at seeing her sister—and missing her— Carrie sent her love before being swarmed by well-wishers.

"Mommy! Mommy!" Katie's voice cut through the crowd. When she got to her mom, she reached and took her hand. "Mommy, is it true? If you marry Uncle Johnny do I get another grandma and grandpa?"

Carrie crouched down to look Katie in the eye, "Katie-girl, when I marry Uncle Johnny you'll get another grandma and grandpa, and uncle and aunty and cousin!"

Katie's eyes were huge. "WHO Mommy? WHO?"

"Uh, over there," Carrie pointed to Tom and Martha who were both talking to Angela.

"Those are Angela's, Mommy!"

"Yes, and they'll be yours too! And Angela will be your cousin, and Max and Jenny will be your Uncle Max and Auntie Jenny."

"But what about Uncle Johnny? What will he be?"

"Well, technically the term is step-dad. We'll have to figure out what we want that to be."

Her voice dropped down to a whisper, "Could he be my Johnny Daddy?"

Carrie had to fight the tears that threatened to spill again, "Yeah Katie-girl. He would love to be your Johnny Daddy."

Satisfied, Katie ran off to tell Angela all about the new arrangements. Carrie felt her mom's hand on her shoulder and turned around to smile through the tears.

The rest of the night passed in a blur as Carrie found out just how hard Jonathan had worked to keep his proposal a secret. Only Matthew, Max, and Jenny's parents had been in on it. *Now* Carrie understood why Tom and Martha had come to her party. They were Jonathan's only family and he wanted them to be a part of the big night.

Feeling arms wrap around her from behind, Carrie turned to see Jenny.

"You've been like a sister to me since the first day you came into my house and rescued me. I couldn't be happier that you're going to be my sister for real!"

Carrie leaned her head on Jenny's arm. "Me too sis, me too."

Finally Carrie couldn't keep her eyes open anymore. "Walk us home?" she asked Jonathan.

"Of course."

She said her goodbyes and thank you's and they made their way back to Carrie's. His hand in hers helped to ground her after such an emotional night. On the other side of Jonathan Katie swung his other hand while singing "Johnny Daddy" over and over.

At the front door he bent to kiss Carrie.

"You guys have done too much kissing tonight!" Katie declared.

"Well, I have to remind your Mommy that she's going to marry me. Kissing's the best way!"

Katie looked at him suspiciously. He reached down and picked her up. "Did you have fun tonight?"

"Yes!"

"Good. Have a good night and I'll come over tomorrow and bring breakfast OK?"

"OK Johnny Daddy!" She gave him a big hug and he put her down before giving Matthew their signature handshake and shoulder bump.

"See you in the morning. And thanks for your help with the proposal!"

Matthew looked at Carrie before turning back to Jonathan. "It made Mom happy. And me too."

Carrie resisted the urge for one more kiss, out of consideration for the kids, but the look Jonathan gave her was almost as good as a kiss.

"Night," she whispered.

"Night."

Carrie tucked in both kids and collapsed into bed. She lay there smiling as she thought back over the last year. Dating Jonathan had confirmed two things: he wasn't perfect—no one was—but he was perfect for her and the kids.

Ahead of her lay two weeks of relaxing (and catching up on housework) before she started her practicum. She'd be working two days a week at the women's shelter downtown where Mary volunteered, and one day a week at the clinic Kara worked at. It had taken some convincing to be approved for both, since she'd have two supervisors that would be reporting back to the program. But in the end she got what she wanted.

Her happiness dimmed a bit as she thought about Don. He had changed tactics after he could no longer bully Carrie, and had gone through the social services system to get access to the kids. With all her friends supporting her, Carrie had sought sole custody in court, but Don succeeded in getting supervised visits. Twice a month Carrie and Jonathan drove the kids to a social worker's office where they waited anxiously in the car until the visit was over. In another year Matthew could refuse to go but he had already said he wouldn't let Katie visit alone.

Her business had covered all Carrie's expenses for the past eight months thanks to her mom's work painting frames, and Lauren's continued success. The time taken to keep the website fresh and ship out orders was less than she had spent working on frames the year before, and she had needed all the extra time to cope with school. Graduating without adding any more debt was a huge source of pride for her.

And now? A wedding to think about. A career to think about. Kids to raise. A whole future to enjoy. It couldn't be this good. Could it? She snuggled further into bed. Yeah, she decided, it could.

A Note From the Author:

I hope you enjoyed *Life Upcycled*! As an independent author I rely on reviews and word of mouth to help promote my work. If you liked this book, please leave a review.

To hear when my next book comes out, please like my author page and you'll be the first to know:

fb.me/CarmenKlassen.Author

May all your days be full of good books, nice people, and happy endings.

Sincerely,

Carmen

Read on for an exclusive sneak preview of Book 4 in the Success on Her Terms series…

Jaz lay motionless in her bed, breathing as shallow as possible. The second she heard the front door close she jumped up and dashed to the bathroom. Kneeling in front of the toilet she threw up. Tears streamed down her face as she felt her body continue to retch. She wasn't stupid. This probably meant the worst thing that could possibly happen. Jasmine Lee, only child, class valedictorian, on the starting line of her volleyball team, and set to start pre-med in September, was pregnant.

She lay down on the cold tile floor for a few minutes before making herself get up. Opening the window and turning on the fan, she got in the shower and sat down. It was too hard to stay standing while her legs were shaking. At exactly 6:45 her mom would return from her morning run, and Jaz would pretend that everything was fine.

Final exams started next week. Then graduation, and the speech she had already written and memorized—before realizing she could be pregnant. After another minute of crying in the shower, she forced herself to stop. Her mom couldn't possibly guess what was wrong, but she'd know that something wasn't right if Jaz came downstairs with red eyes.

Jaz had three things to do today: survive another day of school, go to the walk-in clinic and get a pregnancy test, and hide everything from her parents. No matter what happened next, she would give them their moment to bask in the glory of having a brilliant, popular daughter who was going to be a surgeon before she destroyed their whole world after making one very big mistake. And if she wasn't pregnant, then at least her parents would never know that she had slept with their best friend's 'perfect' son.

A NOTE FROM THE AUTHOR

A Note From the Author:

Thank you for taking the time to read *Life Upcycled*! If you enjoyed it, please consider telling your friends or posting a short review. Word of mouth is an author's best friend and much appreciated! Thank you again!

To be the first to hear when my next book comes out, and for a chance to win bookish prizes, sign-up for my newsletter:

www.carmenklassen.com

And you can like my Facebook author page:

fb.me/CarmenKlassen.Author

May all your days be full of good books, nice people, and happy endings.

Sincerely,

Carmen

READ ON FOR AN EXCLUSIVE SNEAK
PREVIEW OF BOOK 4 …

Jaz lay motionless in her bed, breathing as shallow as possible. The second she heard the front door close she jumped up and dashed to the bathroom. Kneeling in front of the toilet she threw up. Tears streamed down her face as she felt her body continue to retch. She wasn't stupid. This probably meant the worst thing that could possibly happen. Jasmine Lee, only child, class valedictorian, on the starting line of her volleyball team, and set to start pre-med in September, was pregnant.

She lay down on the cold tile floor for a few minutes before making herself get up. Opening the window and turning on the fan, she got in the shower and sat down. It was too hard to stay standing while her legs were shaking. At exactly 6:45 her mom would return from her morning run, and Jaz would pretend that everything was fine.

Final exams started next week. Then graduation, and the speech she had already written and memorized—before realizing she could be pregnant. After another minute of crying in the shower, she forced herself to stop. Her mom couldn't possibly guess what was wrong, but she'd know that something wasn't right if Jaz came downstairs with red eyes.

Jaz had three things to do today: survive another day of school, go to the walk-in clinic and get a pregnancy test, and hide everything from her parents. No matter what happened next, she would give them their moment to bask in the glory of having a brilliant, popular daughter who was going to be a surgeon before she destroyed their whole world after making one very big mistake. And if she wasn't pregnant, then at least her parents would never know that she had slept with their best friend's 'perfect' son.